A Quantum Love
Adventure

Other books by Annie Wood

Dandy Day
A Quantum Love Adventure

A Quantum Love Adventure

Annie Wood

SPEAKING VOLUMES, LLC
NAPLES, FLORIDA
2019

A Quantum Love Adventure

This is a work of fiction. All information, and the words are the author's alone. The publisher does not have any control over and does not assume any responsibility for author or websites or their content.

ISBN 978-1-62815-986-8

Dedicated to the love of all of my lives,
il mio amore,
Peter Arpesella.
Ti amo.
Sempre.

Table of Contents

ITALIA

Staffolo, in the Marche region of Italy, is a picturesque explosion of sunflowers in the summer, with warm weather and blue skies. Each day spent in this little town feels like you've entered a Van Gogh with the paint still wet. Not in a sticky, incomplete way, but in a way that makes you want to spin around in the colors for awhile like a kid set loose with paints during an arts and crafts class. Everyone feels alive here. Happy. An authentic happy. The sort of happy you can actually feel with each inhale and exhale. The sort of happy that you never thought was possible. Especially if you are Martin Stazinski.

Martin is forty going on one-hundred and forty. Martin is certain that nothing great will ever happen to him, so he lives in a permanent state of curmudgeon-dom. When Martin was a boy, his father had a plaque hanging on his office wall that read, *Hope for the Best. Cope with the Rest.* But Martin doesn't believe in the former so he only follows the latter. And sometimes he's not so great at that, either. He knows if he expects nothing, he will never be disappointed. This is Martin's default behavior mode – expect nothing.

Except when Martin is in Staffolo.

Annie Wood

In Staffolo, Martin owns the popular bread-and-breakfast country house, *La Tua Casa,* with his beautiful wife Abby. Here, Martin is magically transformed into an idealistic, positive thinker who is certain that only good things await him.

Martin finishes off his delightful daily pre-lunch cappuccino and helps set the table for *pranzo,* lunch, with his wife. The Italian pop singer Toto Cotugno sings *"Lasciatemi Cantare"* on their little antique radio, while they set out the elegant cloth napkins on the long wood table that sits outside, under a fig tree. Bamboo chimes make their gentle music in the breeze. Under the tree sit two woven baskets full of fresh figs. Abby retrieves the baskets and sets them on the table.

"You told them noon, right?" Martin asks Abby.

"Yep. Angela will be here. She's from Germany, but speaks perfect English. And the Rogersons will definitely be joining us. They're from Boston, so no need to try and impress them with your 'learn a new Italian phrase a day' thing."

Martin responds by showing off the results of his latest lesson. *"Scimmia, lavati I denti!"*

Abby smiles. "*Molto bene, amore mio.* Now if you ever meet an Italian monkey you can tell him to brush his teeth."

Martin tickles Abby, and she wiggles away, laughing. "*Basta!* Our guests will be down any second!"

"So? We should show people from around the world what real love looks like."

Martin holds Abby in his arms. He looks into her eyes, and can't imagine what he must have done right to deserve the love of this beautiful woman and to be able to live in this Italian paradise.

"We'll have plenty of *us* time later. Right now we need to focus on our guests," Abby says.

Martin kisses Abby on the nose. "You are so very difficult to argue with."

"Then don't." Abby kisses him back on his nose. It's one of their terribly cutesy bits they wouldn't dare do in public, but both enjoy immensely.

Stefano, a short, fifty-something Italian man with a limp, approaches the table, holding an armful of sunflowers.

"*Buongiorno!*" Stefano says.

"*Buongiorno! Fiori bellissimi! Grazie,*" says Abby as she takes the flowers and puts them in the vase she's set out on the table.

Stefano is the groundskeeper at *La Tua Casa*. The country home sits on eleven acres and keeping up with all that land is a challenge. Stefano is in charge of overseeing the gardeners and other workers who tend to the abundant plant life, the pool and spa area, and all the outdoor needs. His wife died several years ago in the same accident that caused his leg injury. Martin and Abby hired him shortly thereafter and have helped him, along with his ten-year-old daughter Silvia, through the grieving process.

Silvia skips over to Martin and hands him an extra-large sunflower. He takes it with a dramatic bow and hands it to Abby with a kiss. Abby attempts to put the flower in her hair and then pretends to fall sideways from the weight of it, making Silvia giggle infectiously, declaring that the flower is too large – *"Tropo grande!"* She skips away, nearly knocking over Maria.

Maria is short and stout, just like the tea pot in the song, except not as dainty. Octogenarian Maria helps in the kitchen. She has an apartment in Rome, three hours away by car, give or take, depending how much faster than the speed limit she drives. She enjoys working, so she lends a hand in the kitchen on weekends when *La Tua Casa* is at its busiest. Maria has an opinion about everything. *"Troppa cannella!"* She's waving a jar of fig marmalade in the air, yelling that there's too much cinnamon.

"I was just trying something new, Maria," Abby says. Maria goes on to explain that people, the guests, have grown accustomed to her *fichi* marmalade, *senza* cinnamon, and she is certain that they will be gravely disappointed by its inferior impostor. Martin and Abby always get a kick out of Maria's dramatics.

"Possiamo mettere fuori tutte due le marmellate. La gente puo' scegliere." Abby tells Maria that they can *both* put their marmalades out. That the people can choose. Maria, unconvinced, leaves in a huff. She mumbles that change is not good and people like what they like.

"Cambiamento. Non va bene cambiare troppo. Alla gente non piace cambiare! Mio dio!" Martin thinks that in spite of her dramatics, she does make a good point. Change can be a real pain in the ass.

Abby turns to Martin. "Do you promise to love me even when I'm old and cranky?"

"How cranky and in what language?" Martin says, pulling her in for a kiss. Abby playfully smacks his arm. Martin adds, "I will love you even if you are the Queen of Crank and speak to me only in Swahili."

He holds her in his arms on that sunny, brilliant day under the fig tree, and thinks that life could not possibly get any better than this. Martin remembers in a foggy, faraway way a time when he hated to travel. He remembers when he despised the idea of mingling with others, let alone *hosting* others. He'd never had much of an interest in other cultures or in other languages. Martin had never been into "other" at all. In fact, it's quite surprising that he should find himself here in this time and place.

Yet he finds this particular time and place to be . . . spectacular.

Martin and Abby continue to kiss as the warm wind blows around them. The kiss feels as if it can go on forever. Until . . .

Martin jolts out of bed.

There is no Abby.

No sunflowers.

No Italy.

Martin looks around him.

He's disappointed.

He's distraught.

He's Pissed.

"Craaaaaaaap!"

LOS ANGELES

". . . Craaaaaaap!" Martin is still yelling as he jumps out of his small, sad, single bed. He freezes for a moment. He looks around at his messy apartment in Los Angeles. He's alone. Dean Martin is on the radio singing about pasta fazool.

He groggily gets himself out of his creaky bed, sighing heavily. This is it. Just another day in the real world. Martin makes his way past his video camera, which sits on a chair along with lighting equipment and bounce boards.

As Martin stumbles out of bed to make his way to the kitchen for his morning cup of coffee, he passes by a book on his nightstand. It's an old, antique-looking hardcover. It quietly opens up as if caught by a strong breeze, stopping on page 111. Martin, still trapped in his morning fog, doesn't notice. He glances into his hallway mirror. A tired, middle-aged frump stares back at him. The *before* picture to the *after* picture of the Martin he just saw in Italy.

He finds his way to his sparse kitchen to turn the faucet on, letting the hot water run a long time as his way of heating it up. He knows he could use a kettle or the microwave, but for reasons known only to him, he prefers running the faucet this way.

He goes to the cupboard while the water runs and grabs the instant coffee. He finds his favorite mug, the one with the delightful saying, *Screw this, I'm going back to bed* printed on it. He pours coffee into the mug, eye-balling the correct amount, and then proceeds to catch the now lukewarm faucet water in the mug. He stirs the entire concoction with the back of a steak knife that he found in the sink with the rest of the dirty dishes. Martin takes a long sip of his daily cup of coffee and makes a disgusted face. It's the same face he makes each and every morning after taking his first sip of this tepid-gunk-in-a-mug.

That's Martin's real life, in a nutshell. It's tepid-gunk-in-a-mug. But he still continues to drink it.

Martin's best buddy, Rick, lets himself in the front door. Actually, Rick isn't just Martin's best friend, he's Martin's only friend. He looks exactly like a slightly younger version of Stefano from Martin's dream. Rick plops himself down on the sofa, kicking up a cloud of dust, which makes him cough furiously. After the cough-ing subsides, he places his feet up on the coffee table, knocking over a stack of mail and empty Chinese take-out food containers. Rick starts to mimic the sound of an alarm, "BEEP! BEEP! BEEP!" Martin enters the living room and promptly smacks Rick's feet off the table. "Don't you ever knock?"

"Have I ever knocked?"

"No. You haven't. Why is that?"

"Knocking is so formal. We're buds. Buds don't knock."

"And what's with the beeping?"

"I thought you were still sleeping. I was being your alarm clock."

"Yeah, well, I wake up to music."

"Is that why you're always so delightful? I'd love some coffee, by the way."

Martin hands him his mug. Rick has a sip and promptly spits it out.

"What the hell is this?"

"It's good enough for me," Martin says.

"Maybe you should raise the bar, buddy, because this shit is disgusting." Rick wipes his mouth on his sleeve, shaking his head. Martin feels like an unsolvable puzzle to Rick. But Rick keeps thinking that if he could only find some corner pieces, he could make some headway, even without having the picture on the front of the box to go by. Corner pieces would really be helpful. At least then Rick would have an *outline* to Martin. But even after decades of friendship, none of the pieces have come together to make any sort of recognizable form. So far it's been nothing but sky.

"Why aren't you dressed? We told Professor Welles we'd be at his office at eight sharp. It's seven-thirty now." Rick says.

Martin disappears into his bedroom to get dressed. He yells from there, "I can't understand your obsession with punctuality."

Rick puts his feet back up on the coffee table.

"Of course, you can't. Being on time is for those of us with a sense of responsibility."

"Relax! We won't be late!" Martin yells.

"Hey, what's with you today? You seem grumpier than usual."

"I had a weird dream," Martin says as he comes back into the room, carrying his film equipment. He puts the equipment down and then smacks Rick's feet off the coffee table again. Martin puts his boots on.

"A dream? Is that it? That's easy. Tell it to me and I'll tell you what it means."

"That's just it. I can't exactly remember it."

"Tell me the parts you remember."

Martin closes his eyes and tries to chase any images that may still be lurking in his mind. Just when he thinks he gets a glimpse of something it turns into a white shadow of nothingness. "It's more of a feeling than a memory."

"Fine, tell me what you *felt*. But quickly."

"Italy," Martin says.

"Italy? You *felt* Italy?"

"Si." Martin smiles as he almost remembers.

"You hate to travel," Rick reminds him.

"Well, I didn't do it on purpose."

"Right."

"Anyhow," Martin adds. "It felt good. Real good."

"Good? You're right, that would be a weird sensation for you."

Martin ignores Rick and continues. "And peaceful. Also, it didn't feel like a dream."

"Like when you're not sure if it was real or not?"

"Yeah. Do you ever have those?" Martin is now wearing his boots, so Rick takes this as a sign that he's ready and grabs some of the equipment and heads for the front door.

"Nah, I never remember my dreams." He looks at his watch. "It's seven thirty-six now." Rick opens the door and gestures towards it.

"I think you were there too," Martin says, remembering.

Rick pushes him out the door. "Really? What about the Tin Man? How about the Scarecrow? He's my favorite."

Martin follows Rick out the door. He hears the faint sound of an Italian song and he begins to softly sing along with it.

"What the hell are you doing?" Rick says. Martin snaps out of the moment, stops singing, and continues to walk out with Rick. Rick is talking to him, but all Martin can do is think about the song he just heard. It was all in Italian, but he knew what the lyrics meant.

Good Morning Italy
Good Morning Mother Mary
with eyes full of sadness
Good Morning God
I know you know I am here too.

But since he's never once left Los Angeles County, he can't for the life of him figure out how he could possibly know any of it at all.

THE PROFFESOR

Martin pushes aside the dream he can't remember and concentrates at the job at hand. He and Rick were hired by the brilliant, yet eccentric, quantum physicist, Professor Welles, to shoot a documentary about him. The professor has a large grey mustache that curls up at the ends. He's balding, wears glasses, and speaks in excited, hushed tones as if he's constantly on the edge of revealing something huge. Little children often mistake the professor for a peer. Or a very large baby. The man practically bubbles over with enthusiasm.

He's so giddy with excitement that he often bursts out into laughter for no apparent reason. It's as if he's carrying on a continuous conversation of inside jokes between himself and himself.

Martin interviews Professor Welles off-screen as Rick runs camera. The professor is in the middle of theorizing. He sits behind a large desk, on which there's a bust of a smiling Albert Einstein.

Professor Welles speaks into the camera.

"Einstein didn't much care for chance. Even though quantum mechanics was set into motion by his own early work, Einstein couldn't make it jibe with his idea of how the physical world works. Einstein's theories demand that the universe is orderly and predictable. But, on the scale of atoms and particles, the world is not orderly and predictable. The world is one thrilling, fascinating, mind-blowing game of chance. At the quantum level, *uncertainty* rules." The professor loves this last bit so much he is positively beaming with joy as he puffs on his pipe and smiles wildly into the camera. It would seem that quantum physics really turns this guy on. Also, he loves the attention. His eyes smile too, keeping his mouth company. Tyra Banks calls this *smizing.* The professor is a master smizer. He anxiously waits for Martin to ask him the next question.

"Okay, great. I think we're good for today." Rick stops filming and he and Martin immediately start to pack up their equipment.

"What do you mean? There's so much more to discuss!" The professor pleads, almost as heartbroken as a teenager who was stood up at prom.

"I'm sure there is. But you wanted your cohorts in there too, right? Plus we need room for some fancy visuals or . . . something," explains Martin.

"I like the pipe, Professor." Rick adds, feeling kind of bad for the guy.

The professor loves compliments almost as much as quantum physics, and lights up with another smile.

"Oh, you do? Good! I thought it would add to the overall *professor presence*."

"My gramps used to smoke a pipe. I love the smell," Rick says.

"Oh dear God, I wouldn't dare smoke the damn thing! That stuff will kill you. It's merely a prop that I pretend to puff. I'm quite convincing with the puffing, aren't I?"

"You sure are," Rick agrees.

Professor Welles leans his prop pipe up against the bust of Einstein so it appears as if Einstein is smoking it.

"We can shoot more later if we need to, and if you're available," Martin says.

"I'm available, I'm available," the professor assures him. He watches as his new friends leave his office with their camera and lights. He stares at the Einstein bust and wonders if Einstein would have changed his mind about quantum theory if he were alive today. If so, what would he say to convince Martin to become more interested? WWED? What Would Einstein Do? He leaps out of his chair as if he has suddenly received the answer. The professor sticks his head out of the window and screams down to Martin below.

"Martin, old chum! Did you get a chance to read the book I gave you?"

Martin and Rick crane their necks to look up at the professor. Martin yells back, "I'm not really much of a reader!"

Rick nudges Martin and whispers, "He's our boss, you idiot. *Lie.*"

Martin quickly adds, "But I will give it a try. I promise."

This pleases the professor. He waves goodbye to the guys and moves away from the window. He walks over to Einstein and pats him on the head.

"I'll prove it all to you one day, Al, my boy."

As Martin and Rick pack up the car, Martin realizes that he suddenly has a hankering for *caprese*, even though he's lactose intolerant and never much cared for basil. He can smell the balsamic vinegar as if someone passed a bottle under his nose. Up until this moment he didn't even know that he knew the ingredients that made up *caprese*.

"I can't get into all of that mumbo-jumbo metaphysical stuff," Martin says, slamming the trunk shut. It's always such a shockingly pleasant surprise when his camera and lighting equipment, bounce boards and sound equipment all fit into the back of his beat-up, exhausted 1991 Toyota Celica. It all has to find its way inside amongst the fast food wrappers, old shoes, and dirty towels from God knows when. Martin's sloppiness is not limited to his apartment and personal grooming.

"It's *science*," Rick reminds him.

"It's quantum *Loony Tunes* science."

"I think it's interesting."

"Look, I'm doing this for the payday and that's all. Faking actual interest will cost extra." Martin leans against his car. "How did you get this gig for us anyway?"

"Through the kick-ass website I designed for us."

"That's it? He just hired us straight from a website?"

"It's a good website," Rick says.

"It's not that good."

"Don't be a hater. Seriously, we should actually spend more time with Professor Welles. He's like one of the leaders in Loony Tunes science."

"Rick, what's my motto?"

Rick has heard Martin's motto a million times.

Rick quotes Martin in his monotone, exhausted way, *"Never do more than is absolutely necessary."*

"Exactly!" Martin walks around to the driver's seat and gets into his car.

Rick leans in. "Hey, let's grab some breakfast."

"Oh. I can't." He tries to follow it up with reasons why he can't grab breakfast with his friend, but the only real reason is that Martin knows that he'd be lousy company and he doesn't want to bring Rick down. He thinks that would sound too much like self-pity talk to say aloud. "I'm just going to go home and start the edit."

"Now? Can't it wait?" Rick asks.

"The sooner I start, the sooner we have a finished product for the professor, and the sooner we get paid."

Rick senses that Martin could use some company but if he leaves now he can catch his wife and kids in time so he can surprise them with a day of mini-golf.

"So, are you saying the Rickster is no longer needed at this juncture?" he asks Martin.

Martin nods, and Rick hops to it.

"Okay. See you later!" Rick takes off for his car, sprinting the whole way. He's a man who really enjoys his wife, his kids, and mini-golf.

Martin watches Rick sprint and wishes he had someone to sprint home to. Not that he enjoys sprinting, that's too much work. But maybe if he had someone to sprint to, it wouldn't feel like work. He shakes his head quickly, as if he had a sudden chill, trying to shake off the blues. He turns the radio on, thinking the music can energize him enough to get him home.

The first station he finds has Gilbert O'Sullivan singing about being alone again. Martin is not amused. The next song has Elvis asking him if he's lonesome tonight. He thinks about smashing his fist against the radio but decides against it. Changes the radio station again and its

Roy Orbison claiming that only the lonely know why I cry. "Seriously?" Martin punches the radio. "Owww."

He rolls down the window, thinking that the fresh air might do him some good. It can't be any worse than how the music just treated him.

Inside a passing Prius, he notices a young girl sitting in the backseat. The girl is wearing a hat with a huge sunflower on the top of it. She smiles and waves. Martin is not the type to wave at strangers, child or not, but this girl feels so . . . familiar. He lifts up his hand to wave, and then speeds up to get a look at the little girl's parents. Maybe he knows them somehow. This thought seems just as strange as Martin knowing the kid, because Martin doesn't get out much. Sure enough, the parents don't seem familiar at all. He slows the car down and glances into the backseat of the car again to have another look at the girl. It's that hat of hers. She's smiling and waving at him like she knows him. Then it hits him. She's the same girl who gave him the sunflower in his dream. He hears her giggle as if she was inside the car right there with him at that very moment.

Stress. I'm stressed out, that's it. But stress from what? Life in general. Stress from life in general is totally a thing. The Prius makes a sharp right at the light and slowly disappears as the little girl presses her face up against the back window, sadly waving goodbye to Martin. She mouths, *"Ciao."*

    That was weird, Martin thinks to himself. *Really weird.*

COSMIC

It's late at night and Martin is in his dank apartment living room seated in front of his computer. He's in the midst of editing the footage he has gathered for this "Loony Tunes science" project. Quantum physicists, each one kookier than the last, appear on the screen and speak into the camera.

"Because, you see, the universe is infinite, due to *cosmic inflation*, the universe is much bigger than it was at its inception," says Doctor Stevens. Martin fast forwards and lands on Professor Sally Figgins.

"Strings! That's what it's all about! String theory is the notion that all particles are made up of vibrating strings."

Martin fast forwards again, stopping on Dr. Lee. "Bubbles! Big, awesome, *cosmic bubbles*. That's where all the universes live! Making the universe really a *multiverse*. All parallel universes fit *inside* of these floating bubbles, including ours."

Martin has had enough. He pushes pause and heads to the kitchen for a snack. He mumbles on the way over to the fridge, "Strings and bubbles." His eyes search the fridge side to side, top to bottom. There's one lone string cheese on the middle rack, and one can of Mountain Dew on the bottom rack.

"Strings," he says as he reaches for the string cheese. "And bubbles," he adds as he reaches for the Mountain Dew. "How freakin' cosmic."

As Martin settles in for his cosmic snack, he texts Rick.

professor's friends are a bunch of talking heads. need to liven it up. graphics? animators? FX?

After a few moments Rick texts back.

disneyland with the fam.

list of graphic artists at home.

take a break.

talk 2morrow.

Martin does his best Scrooge impression and bah-humbugs to himself, "Disneyland."

Feeling bored and restless, Martin picks up a maga-zine and flips through the pages. He stops on an ad for hamburger buns. Not because he has a craving for ham-burgers, but because of something else in the photo that he craves. The photo is of a happy family enjoying their day in the backyard. Dad is grilling hamburgers, smiling his satisfied dad-smile, while mom carries a tray of lemonade, smiling her happy mom-smile. The kids play a game of catch nearby. Martin wonders briefly what that might feel like. Enjoying his family on a lazy, sunny

Sunday afternoon. Bothered by his own intrusive thoughts reminding him of what he doesn't have, he tosses the magazine on the table.

He spends the next several minutes stacking a roll of pennies on the coffee table. He then accidentally bumps the coffee table and watches as the pennies come tumbling down. Martin's never been good at busying himself. Unless he has actual work to do, he gets lost. But he's afraid of getting lost in his thoughts. His thoughts and memories are often cruel and unsettling, so he usually just keeps working. He presses play and this time it's the professor on the screen. It's part of the interview Martin and Rick did earlier in the day.

"Cosmic bubbles, string theory, M theory, Heisenburg's uncertainty principle, $E=MC2$ . . . so much noise, isn't it? I mean, much progress has been made in the area of quantum mechanics, and of course I find it all fascinating. To a point." The professor leans in and addresses Martin.

"You know what I like to do, Martin?"

"What?" says Martin from the video.

"What?" repeats Martin from his living room.

"I like to lie down on my couch, right over there. Close my eyes and . . . sleep."

"Are you saying that's when you get your best ideas?" asks video Martin.

"I'm saying that nothing is for certain except that which we *experience.*"

"I'm not sure I'm following you."

"Try it. Relax your mind, relax your body, and let yourself take in all that you've read, heard, all that you know, or more accurately, *think* that you know. And then allow yourself to . . . experience the truth."

"Experience the truth." Martin repeats. "Whatever the hell that means." The footage continues rolling as Martin's eyelids get heavier and heavier.

The professor looks straight into the camera and giggles, "Try it. It's a trip."

BELLISSIMO

Martin is still sleeping on his sofa in the same position he was in when he first fell asleep to the sound of the professor's voice.

Except it's not the same sofa.

It's not the same living room.

"Wake up, sleepy head," whispers Abby as she snuggles up against him. The sun is shining in through the large bay windows. Chimes blow in the breeze, and Martin cozies up with the hand-knitted throw that he finds wrapped around him. He looks as serene as a coddled baby. Abby watches him for a moment. She remembers how an ex once told her how he liked her best when she was sleeping. Which she found outrageously obnoxious. She told him that it was easy to like someone when they're sleeping, because there's no threat or possibility of conflict of any kind. But Abby doesn't like Martin best when he's sleeping she just likes how calm he feels.

"Martin, time to get up. We have to set up colazione."

He opens his eyes and sees the beautiful Abby smiling down at him. He smiles at first and then he jolts out of bed as if a lightning bolt just sizzled right through him.

"What the hell happened?" Martin panics.

"Nothing happened. You just seemed so out of it after dinner last night. Maybe too much vino."

"I don't remember having any wine," Martin says, confused.

"Really? Because you certainly made a big show of it in front of our guests. It was the Rosso Conero you picked up in town. You promised them it was *il miglior vino del mondo.*"

"I said what now?"

"Do you have an ear prompter in your ear on the nights you speak Italian? How can you forget the very next day?"

"I'm . . . not sure. And what guests?"

"Oh, I get it," she teases. "You want to play 'amnesia victim.' Okay, Mr. Stazinski, does this bring back any memories?" Abby leans in and kisses Martin softly. Martin is transfixed by her beauty and doesn't want to rock the boat, but he needs to make sense of this.

"I had the strangest dream," he tells her.

"Another woman?" Abby jokes.

"No. Not another woman."

"Another man? Oh, Martin, how European of you."

"No, no . . . not that kind of a dream."

"Okay, so tell me the dream," she says, squeezing in next to him.

"I can't really remember now. Shoot. I had it . . . then we started talking and I lost it."

"If I had a nickel every time I heard that line." Abby laughs. An adorable terrier mix jumps up on Martin. "Hey there, little guy."

"Nice timing, Professor," Abby tells the dog.

"Professor?" Martin asks.

"What? *You* named him."

"Yeah . . . I know." Martin says, faking a memory of naming the dog and faking a memory of the dog itself.

"You love him, right?" Abby asks hopefully.

"Sure. Of course." Professor licks Martin's face.

"We have so much room here and you promised that after a year, if we stayed in Italy and if we kept the inn, we could get a dog. So when Professor followed Stefano into the giardino ieri you said it was meant to be. Ti ricordi?"

"The garden . . . Yesterday . . . *Si, si*, of course I remember." His Italian is now coming back to him, but not much else. Martin can't even remember ever having gotten a passport, let alone the traveling itself.

"We're keeping him," Martin declares.

Professor barks enthusiastically.

"Great! Now, let's get ready for colazione. It's almost eight," Abby says, bouncing up and heading for the cucina with Professor shadowing her happily.

27

Annie Wood

Martin rubs his temples as he slowly follows behind. He feels like he needs to remember something important, but he also feels like he'd rather not. Maybe he really does have amnesia. Although he read somewhere that amnesia is fairly rare, happening much more in movies and on television than it does in real life. And this *is* real life, isn't it? Martin finds the kitchen and watches as Abby sets up an impressive spread of freshly-baked cakes and croissants, each one looking and smelling better than the last. *Who cares if it's real,* Martin thinks. *I'm staying.*

As Silvia helps carry plates with Maria she sneaks a biscotti. Maria catches her and snaps out her usual rant which always makes Silvia giggle.

"Non ti diamo da mangiare qui? Serviti dopo, non prima degli ospiti!"

Silvia notices Martin watching. She smiles and rushes over to him to give him a big hug. *"Buongiorno, zio Martin!"*

Martin's never been much of a hugger or a kid person yet here he is hugging this kid who refers to him as *Uncle* Martin. Professor runs around happily, following Abby as she brings Martin a cup of coffee. He has a sip and is dumbstruck.

"This is insanely good."

Abby, confused by Martin's enthusiastic response over his usual cup of coffee is about to ask him what's

28

different about it, but the guests begin to trickle in. Each one is smiling ear to ear and thanking Martin and Abby for being such gracious hosts, telling them how much they enjoyed dinner last night and what a beautiful inn this is and they will be sure to tell all of their friends back home that they must visit *La Tua Casa*. Martin smiles and nods as he walks, in a daze, through the kitchen and into the giardino.

"Martin's a little out-of-it before his first cappuccino," Abby explains to her guests.

Martin takes a deep breath and takes it all in. The air is so insanely fresh that he can barely breathe from the shock of it. The sunflowers, yes, he remembers the sunflowers from the other dream. Or is it from the other day? There's a flock of birds happily singing their morning songs. The bougainvillea crawls up the side of the home. The home, his home, *La Tua Casa, Your Home.*

Is this my place? Martin wonders, really hoping that it is. The place is surrounded by olive trees, and the smell of the figs from the fig tree has a sweet familiarity to it. He looks inside to find Abby laughing with their guests. Professor is on her lap now, cuddled up and content.

Martin has a feeling wash over him that he doesn't quite recognize; complete and total contentment.

"Come on!" Abby calls to him. "Maria made your favorite. Nutella torta!"

Martin stares at Abby as if hypnotized for a second. "Come!" Abby repeats, and he walks back inside the *cucina*. He's not entirely sure what Nutella torta is but he knows he wants some.

Maria brings him a slice of cake as Martin sits with his guests. He speaks in part Italian and part English, the Italian coming to him out of nowhere. He is loosening up a bit and enjoying colazione with everyone. He tells jokes. He shares stories. He's enjoying their company and they're certainly enjoying his. He's remembering more now, little by little. This is what he wanted. What they wanted. They dreamed of moving to Italy and opening up a B&B, and this is what they're doing. They are living the dream.

Unless he's not living. Unless he's dreaming.

With that last thought Martin looks around, trying to see where the ringing cell phone is. It sounds like it's coming from somewhere far away.

"Is that your phone?" Martin asks Abby.

"Phone? I don't hear anything," Abby says.

The phone gets louder and louder.

"Seriously, someone should get that," Martin says, looking at Maria.

Maria responds, declaring her hearing to be perfect and that there's no phone ringing. *"Il mio udito e' perfetto! Il telefono non sta suonando."*

Martin gets up now, frantically looking for the phone. The dog senses Martin's agitation and cocks his head to the side while the guests stare, unsure of what's going on. Martin covers his ears with his hands. The noise is just too much. Just when he thinks he can't stand it anymore . . .

Martin wakes up.

In his crappy bed.

In his crappy apartment.

In Los Angeles.

Alone.

DREAMER

Martin bounces out of his bed. He reaches for the ringing cell sitting on the bedside table.

"What?"

"Well, a jolly good morning to you too, ol' pal."

"Rick. What time is it?"

"Most people find the clocks they keep by their bedside helpful in moments like this."

"I can't trust my eyes. They've been seeing all sorts of weird things lately."

"It's nine-thirty. Did you have a long night?"

"Night? I slept through the night?"

"That's what big boys do sometimes."

Martin brings the phone into the bathroom and puts it on speaker while he splashes cold water on his face.

"What's that sound? Hey! Are you peeing? Oh, man, don't pee and talk to me at the same time. You know I hate that."

"Relax. It's just the faucet." Martin dries his face and takes the phone with him into the living room. The screen is still on from the night before, frozen on the professor's mischievous grin. It's as if the professor is smiling directly through Martin. Martin finds this a bit creepy, yet he can't look away.

"So, I have that number for the graphic artist," Rick informs him.

"Actually, this stuff is pretty interesting after all."

"I thought you didn't believe in all of that Loony Tunes mumbo-jumbo."

"I had another dream," Martin blurts.

"The good-feeling dream?" Rick asks.

"Yeah."

"Then how come you don't sound so good?"

"Because I woke up."

"Was I in this one?" Rick asks.

"No."

"How did I look?"

"I said you weren't in this one."

"Bummer."

"And I think you have a limp."

"I thought you said I wasn't in it."

"Well, you didn't *look* like the guy in the dream but you sort of *felt* like him. You're Italian."

"Cool."

"And you have a limp."

"Not cool. Can I get a better part in your next one?"

"I'm not controlling this, Rick. Don't you get it?"

"No, I can't say that I do, buddy."

Martin explains what he knows so far. He goes on to tell Rick how the dream felt like his normal life, but that he was a bit confused in it. Like he was groggy from not sleeping well or something. Then when he woke up in Los Angeles and realized he had only been dreaming, he was disappointed but understood that *this* is real life and *that* was dream life. But then the next time when he was there it felt like *that* was real life, and when he woke up in Los Angeles he felt horrible, as if someone had abruptly ended an incredible trip he was on.

"But you hate traveling."

"Will you quit saying that? I know I hate traveling. Don't you think I know that?"

The last time Martin's mind was on the brink of explosion like this, was when his parents took him to Griffith Observatory for the Pink Floyd laser show. He remembers sitting there at the observatory, feeling like what he imagined being on certain drugs would feel like, only better because there were no pesky side effects to speak of. Now, he has this thing. And this thing is a weird thing. It's an unexplainable thing. But at least it's *some-*thing. He wants to talk about it because if he can't be at *La Tua Casa* with Abby, then the next best thing is talking about being at *La Tua Casa* with Abby.

"Let's go get a drink," Martin says.

"A drink? It's not even ten in the morning, my friend. Besides, me and the fam are about to head out to the farmer's market."

"Oh, right." Martin remembers.

Rick, sensing the loneliness in Martin's voice once again, suggests that Martin come with them. Martin responds with his usual, "Oh, no, no, I have tons of stuff to do."

Both men are quiet for a while. Martin remembers reading somewhere that women do this sort of thing, talk on the phone and then share a bit of silence for whatever reason, but not men. Men need to stay on-point. So the current state of silence isn't welcomed.

Rick doesn't want to abandon his pal, and Martin doesn't want to be abandoned.

In order to break the silence, Rick searches his mind for something else to say.

"Hey," bursts out of Rick's mouth. "Susan ran into Elizabeth the other day."

"Oh, yeah?"

"Yeah. She asked about you. Why don't you give her a call?"

"Nah, she's busy with her family and everything."

"You're her family too."

"Sure. But . . . It's just . . . I have . . ."

Rick finishes the sentence for Martin, ". . . tons of stuff to do. I know, I know." They both can tell that they're bound for another lull in the conversation, and not wanting to risk living through another one of those, Rick quickly adds, "I'll text you later about the film, cool?"

"Cool," Martin agrees and hangs up the phone.

As soon as Rick taps the end button on his cell, he looks around his house. It's a colorful, warm home bursting with energy. He spends a few moments watching his wife chase their giggling kids around. Rick feels a deep sense of appreciation for them, thankful that's he's not alone in this world.

Martin sits on his sofa and surveys his apartment as if he's waiting for something. Maybe if he stares at the walls long enough the walls will speak to him and tell him what he should do next. Maybe his TV set has sage advice and his unmade bed has wisdom to share. But, alas, his apartment and inanimate objects remain selfishly mute. Finally his eyes fall on the professor's frozen gaze on the monitor and Martin feels a profound sense of responsibility. To what or to whom, he's not sure. So as not to become frozen in this sense of not-knowing, Martin proceeds to his kitchen and goes through his familiar daily steps.

- Step 1. Check fridge.
- Step 2. Notice fridge is empty.
- Step 3. Close fridge.
- Step 4. Run tap water to get it warm.

- Step 5. Grab dirty, chipped mug from sink.
- Step 6. Get instant coffee from cupboard.
- Step 7. Plop spoonful of instant coffee into cup.
- Step 8. Retrieve steak knife from dirty sink.
- Step 9. Add hot(*ish*) tap water to cup with coffee.
- Step 10. Stir with back of knife.
- Step 11. Drink very quickly so as not to taste this crappy warm beverage he calls coffee.

Martin remembered a meme he saw of a sunset with the words below it, *take time to enjoy the simple things*. Martin did not heed the advice of this meme. He has never, not once, taken the time to enjoy the simple things. Nor does he make an effort to make the simple things more enjoyable. He just muddles through his days in the safety nook of his low expectations.

He notices that his table is overflowing with mail. Bills, mostly, and magazines he never subscribed to. Martin hates it when magazine companies send him a "free trial" with the intention of suckering him into purchasing a year, or better yet, a lifetime subscription of something he never asked for in the first place. Like these people assume that their magazine is so irresistible that even though one may not have a proclivity towards, say, pottery, after reading a six-week free trial of Pottery Now one will suddenly be hooked and won't be able to bear the end of the trial, thus subscribing to Pottery Now forever and ever amen. Because that's how life works. You don't know how badly you want something until you have it for a little while and then someone threatens to take it away. You don't know what you got till it's gone. Just ask Joni Mitchell.

Also on this table of bills and magazines sits the AARP newsletter. Martin didn't ask for that either. Maybe because he's forty years old and AARP isn't supposed to be of interest until you're "of a certain age." Retirement age. Sixty-five and over feels like the right time to be an AARP target. Although Martin does *feel* like a one-hundred year-old man, how do the AARP people know that? He really hates those freaking newsletters who see through him and into his real-age. But on top of the pile sits one piece of mail that could, that *should,* be of interest to Martin. The envelope has a return address of Indie Filmmaker's Grant.

Open Immediately. Time Sensitive Material.

Martin stares at the envelope but his body can't move to open it. He's aware that it could be good news, but a gnawing voice whispers, *It never is.* Martin stares at the envelope and considers throwing it away unopened, along with the free-trial magazines, the bills, and that asshole

AARP newsletter. But before he can do anything his ringing telephone distracts him. He lets the machine pick up.

He listens to his voice in his less-than-friendly outgoing message:

Not here. Talk now.

He wonders if he could put a little smile in his voice, the way he's heard voice-over actors do. He knows that he probably can't fake a smile convincingly enough, so he lets the outgoing message remain direct, to the point, *senza* smile.

Hey, big bro, It's Elizabeth again. Are you there? I still can't believe you have an answering machine.

Where did you find it, anyway, at an antique store? Anyhow, I've left six messages on your cell. Check in once in a while, will ya?

Hope you're okay. Love you.

Elizabeth is two years younger than Martin. She's always been the brave one. The free spirit. She's the kind of person who doesn't back away from life when things get tough. They got along great as kids, with no sibling rivalry that he can remember. Maybe because she's a girl, or maybe because she's an easy person to love. After their parents death Martin closed himself off to the world and especially to her. Elizabeth looks so much like their mom that it was just too painful to be around her. Martin knows this is a wussy, immature move. But he was just a child when he first made this subconscious choice, and by the time he was no longer a child it felt like that ship had sailed and Elizabeth had moved on. She married her high school sweetheart and started a life of her own. Still, she always checks in. Maybe one day he can show up for her. But probably not.

Feeling restless, Martin makes his way into his bedroom. He opens the closet door, thinking that it might be a good idea to eventually get out of his boxer shorts and t-shirt. He eyes his clothing. He has nothing but jeans and t-shirts. That's it. He doesn't even own a t-shirt with an ironic saying on it. Just plain black t-shirts and blue jeans. He suspects that most of his clothes aren't even clean, since he can't remember the last time he did a load of laundry. Martin stops in the middle of his mess, his eyes and shoulders sagging with resignation. "Maybe I'm not . . . winning life."

Maybe if he could take a nap. Naps are good for you, he hears. All the greats napped. Winston Churchill, John F. Kennedy, Thomas Edison, they all claimed that even short naps recharged them immensely. Also, it's something to do. Ironically, it's doing without doing.

Martin sits down on his unmade bed and lies back. He glances over at the open book the professor gave him. Strange, he doesn't remember opening it. He picks up the book and notices that it's opened to page 111. His mom would always say "make a wish" whenever the digital clocks were at 1:11 or 11:11. Martin imagines that Elizabeth says the same to her son.

He reads a passage from the open page.

Only by exploring beyond our physical limits can we ever hope to comprehend the essence of ourselves and our universe.

Whatever the hell that means.

He closes the book and flips it over to look at the title:

More than Meets the Eye: Parallel Lives and Out-of-Body Experiences by Professor Joseph Welles.

It would appear that the professor didn't just recommend this book.

He wrote it.

ABBY

Staffolo, along with Abby, seemed to have drifted away from Martin. They're a faint memory now, like the outline of the sun after you close your eyes. Brief, glowing images of something that was once there. This makes Martin more agitated than usual. He walks down the street thinking about why he's so annoyed and why those dreams were so real. Why had they seemed to matter so much, as if they were actually happening? What purpose could any of this serve? Martin doesn't enjoy not understanding things. He prefers to know what's what at all times, so he can quickly make a judgment about whether or not the ideas can take up residence in his mind. He doesn't have time for bullshit. Although, truth be told, he's not terribly busy, so he actually does have plenty of time for plenty of bullshit. He walks faster, pestered by his own thoughts. His mind feels foggy. He hasn't felt quite like himself lately.

He passes by the bakery he always walks by, but for the first time he notices a bamboo wind chime blowing in the breeze. The sound of the chimes is familiar but as if it were from another time and place. "Oh, shit . . ." Martin mumbles as he realizes the bamboo chimes are the exact same ones from his dream. This realization gives him an odd, comforting feeling. He looks down and sees that below the chimes sit two woven baskets which also feel oddly familiar. Then he remembers that they too were in his dream. Martin figures that since he has passed this bakery before he must have noticed the chimes and the baskets, which his mind simply transported into his dreams. They are merely traveling memory props.

Martin's pace picks up a bit as he speed-walks past a flower shop called Abby's Flowers. The "O" in "flowers" is in the shape of a sunflower.

Abby.

Sunflowers.

It's coming back to him in lightning bolt visions.

Abby's beautiful face.

The country home.

The sunflowers.

Suddenly his entire life with Abby is as clear as day and a powerful feeling overtakes him.

"I miss you, Abby," slips out of his mouth. How could he feel this intensely for something, someone, who isn't real?

~~~

"Do we know an Abby?" Martin asks Rick, doubled over panting after having ran all the way to the farmer's market to find Rick and his family. Rick, surprised to see him, looks at him quizzically. Martin repeats the question. "*Abby.* Do we know anyone named Abby?"

Rick's pregnant wife, Susan, and their two little boys, Jack and Jerry, watch as Martin tries to catch his breath.

"Glad you could make it," Rick says.

"Did you know that he *wrote* the book?" Martin says, still out of breath.

"What book?"

"The book that the professor keeps pressuring me to read!"

"You know, Martin, we are doing a documentary on the guy, so you might want to research him a bit and read the damn thing."

"Hi, Martin." Susan waves.

Martin is walking in small circles pacing in miniature.

"He seemed to really want me to read it but he didn't want to tell me that he wrote. Like he wanted me to figure it out myself. Like he's trying to tell me something without actually telling me something."

"My wife said hello to you," Rick says.

"What?" Martin has always liked Susan and feels a bit like a jerk for his current state of self-absorption.

"Oh, hi. Sorry, Susan." He kisses her on the cheek. "You look . . ."

Susan puts her hand on her pregnant belly. "Huge. Yeah, I know."

Martin is sweating now and not making eye contact with anyone. He's looking around as if he can find his missing bits and pieces wandering about somewhere at the farmer's market.

"Are you having some sort of mental breakdown? Do I need to call someone?" Rick asks.

"Did we know an Abby growing up?"

"Oh. So we're back to that. No. Not that I can remember."

"Think!" Martin insists. "In school. In one of our classes? Maybe a few years behind."

"Not ringing any bells. Why?"

Martin sighs heavily. "There's a woman in my dreams named Abby."

Rick laughs. "Is that what this is all about? You're having dreams about a woman and that's got you all cuckoo?"

"I'm asking you a simple question."

"No. I don't remember an Abby. Martin, I tell you, if you just got out more you'd meet some *actual* women. Some of them might even still be there when you wake up in the morning."

"What's she like?" asks Susan.

"Babe, please don't encourage him."

Martin, happy to tell someone, turns to Susan and gushes. "She's wise, kind, funny and the most beautiful woman I've ever seen."

"Yeah, I hear that's how they make 'em in dreamland," Rick says.

Susan smacks Rick on the arm.

Rick quickly adds, "I mean, in real life too. That's how they make them in real life too."

"You better say that, or I'll have to move in with this baby's real father," Susan says.

"It wasn't a dream," Martin tells them both in all sincerity.

They look at him, confused. Rick is about to say something when Martin notices a familiar dog running by.

"Professor!" Martin yells after the dog as he takes off to chase it, running once again.

"What's wrong with Uncle Martin?" asks Jerry.

Rick shrugs. "Nobody knows, son. Nobody knows."

THE BOOK

Martin sits alone in an oversized leather chair, waiting for Professor Welles to arrive. He stares at the bust of Einstein. Today there's a red, green and white scarf tied around Einstein's head. The colors of the Italian flag.

Professor Welles storms in like Jumanji.

"Martin, Martin, Martin, such a pleasure! Where's Rick? Where's the camera?"

Martin's anxiety is bursting at the seams, but it can't hold a candle to the professor's enthusiasm over having company and another opportunity to tell his story. Any story, really.

"No camera. Just me today," Martin says quickly.

"No camera?" the professor pouts. "I wore this tie for the camera. I find the color exciting."

"Yeah, it's a very exciting tie. Look, I have questions." Martin leans in, intensely.

The professor mirrors his moves by leaning in to face him. "You want to talk about your dreams, don't you?"

"How did you know that?"

"Didn't you just tell me that?"

"No."

"Oh. Well, I must be hearing things. What would you like to know?" The professor smiles again.

"You're right. I do want to talk about a dream I'm having."

"I don't believe in them."

"Excuse me?"

"If you're looking for a dream analysis you'll need to go to a shrink. Maybe someone adept in the teaching of Freud. Or perhaps a psychic."

"A psychic?"

"I, on the other hand, don't believe that we dream."

"But isn't there scientific proof that we dream?"

"There is proof of activity, yes."

"Well then, I would like to talk about my *activities.*"

"What about them?"

"My activities lately have been especially . . . active."

The professor lights up with pleasure. "A spontaneous experience! Fantastic! What a joy! We will have to work at it a bit for it to continue."

"Work on what?"

The professor continues, now hopping around his office, full of excitement. "This is wonderful! You must be waking up!"

"No, I'm *sleeping* when this happens. I'm dreaming. Why do I get the feeling that you're not listening to me?"

"Did you read the book I gave you?" the professor asks.

"I skimmed it."

"Oh, I'm afraid your skimming days are over." The professor gets up abruptly and walks to the door. He turns around with a flourish and grins at Martin,

"Read it. I think you'll like it."

Pages, words, sentences float across Martin's mind as he lie in bed.

You are in a state of consciousness similar to a twilight between sleep and full waking awareness.

To find the answers, simply tell yourself, 'I will now have an out-of-body experience.' Trust. Let go. Explore!

If the professor wants to play games with him, then fine, he'll play along. Just the mere chance of seeing Abby again is worth feeling stupid for a minute while he's alone in his bedroom. Without much feeling, he repeats the mantra . . .

"I will now have an out-of-body experience. I will now have an out-of-body experience."

He's getting sleepy, but he manages to repeat the sentences with a tad more commitment.

"I will *now* have an out-of-body experience.

I will now have an . . ."

At that moment Martin hears a loud POP. His body begins to vibrate violently. He watches, in utter amazement, as his spirit *actually detaches* as a carbon-copy of his physical body. His spirit self looks down upon his physical self, which is still in bed, motionless. This fact freaks out the spirit self which, in turn, startles the physical self. The sudden fear of both selves makes the physical self quickly suck the spirit self back into him like a high-powered-spirit Hoover.

"WHAT THE FUCK WAS THAT?"

A bewildered Martin stumbles into the bathroom to splash cold water on his face and reassure his reflection in the mirror. "You're cool. It's cool. "

He takes a deep breath. No one said that this dream travel, time travel, or whatever the hell he's attempting to do would be easy. If he wants to see Abby again he better man-up. He's got to pull himself up by the boot straps. Tighten the drawstrings of his pajama pants and make this happen. Martin makes his way back to his bed and climbs back in it for a take-two.

He closes his eyes and chants, "I will now have an out-of-body experience. I will now have an out-of-body experience. I will now have an out-of-body experience."

POP! Body vibrates. Martin's spirit self detaches again, same as before. The physical self tries to suck him back in . . . but the spirit self seems stronger this time. The spirit self steps out of the physical self altogether.

The spirit self looks down at the physical self and speaks to it telepathically. "Stay!"

As soon as the telepathic thought is thought, Martin's spirit self flies straight through the ceiling and into the night sky.

As Martin flies he looks down at the rooftops of his neighbors' homes and laughs with delight. He's freakin' Superman! His spirit self soars. Finally feeling relaxed, he closes his eyes and enjoys it.

But suddenly Martin finds himself on solid ground, driving a car down the highway. He looks like his normal self but he doesn't feel like he's in L.A. or Italy. Pamela, an angry looking middle-aged woman, is sitting in the passenger seat. Martin is in a daze, the way a person might be when they find themselves flying in the sky as a spirit one moment and then driving in a car with an angry woman the next. He swerves suddenly, nearly missing an oncoming truck.

Pamela shrieks. "Martin! What is wrong with you? I told you to move over! Didn't you hear me, you idiot?!"

Martin looks over at this woman, in shock. He recognizes her now. "Pammy? Is that you?"

She stops shrieking for a moment and looks at him with something that almost, but not quite, resembles sweetness. "Pammy? You haven't called me that since the tenth grade."

Pamela and Martin dated in high school until Martin grew a pair and left her and her controlling ways. When Martin explained that he couldn't afford the "going together" ring that Pamela coveted, she convinced him to steal cash from his own grandmother's purse because she should mean more to him then his old grandmother, who won't be around nearly as long as she, and this was how he could prove his everlasting love to Pamela. He proved the opposite by breaking up with Pamela two days before prom. At least, he thought he did. What the hell is he doing driving her anywhere?

A little boy's whining voice from the backseat screams, "When do we stop?"

Another child, another whine, "I want a FroYo!"

And yet another one, louder than all the others, "I have to poop!"

Why is he chauffeuring these brats around? He looks over at Pamela. She was a ball-buster in high school but she was damn cute. Now she's apparently just held on to the ball-busting part of the equation.

"You look so . . . different," he tells her, his eyes lingering too long on her midsection.

She grabs her own stomach flesh hastily. "You mean this souvenir I got from popping out your little monsters through my vagina?"

It appears that he's offended her. And it would also appear that those little monsters were the fruit of his very own loins. At that moment the loudest kid spits a loogie on the closed window and screams again, "I HAVE TO MAKE A POOOP!" *Bad loins. Very bad loins,* Martin thinks.

Martin remembers that closing his eyes brought him here, so maybe closing his eyes can bring him out of here. He closes his eyes. Pamela yells, "What the hell are you doing? Pull the car over this instant!"

He swerves the car, narrowly missing a cyclist this time. Okay, this sucks, he doesn't want to kill anyone, in dreamville or otherwise. He pulls the car over. Pamela gets out of the car and walks around to switch seats with Martin, but she's none too pleased about it.

"I have to do everything! Not a minute to myself! You'd think you could at least drive the damn car without getting us killed!"

Martin can't take it any longer. "GET ME OUT OF HERE, PROFESSOR!" Martin screams at the top of his lungs.

And . . . POP! Just like that, Martin is flying through the air. He looks down and notices that his body is there still being screamed at by Pamela but he is *also* now soaring through the air. He seems to have mastered the whole spirit-leaving-the-body-thing, he realizes as he zooms about at warp speed. He closes his eyes shut and then . . . POP! He's off again!

When Martin opens his eyes again he finds himself in the middle of a sunflower field. Professor, the dog, is licking his face.

"I made it!" Martin says as he scoops up Professor and kisses him on his snout.

The dog barks, wiggles out of Martin's arms and runs off. When Martin looks up, he can see Abby far away in the distance. He waves frantically. He must get to her. He starts running towards her, but the more he runs the further away she appears. "Oh, no . . ." He starts to worry as he keeps trying to run. "Have I fallen into a night-mare?" Abby vanishes. Martin stops running and screams, "What am I doing wrong?" His voice echoes in the air. He closes his eyes in despair and immediately hears the POP and he's off again, leaving the sunflower fields behind, soaring through the clouds as another version of him remains in the fields.

The next time he opens his eyes he finds himself seated at a kitchen table. Not just any kitchen table, but the one he grew up eating breakfast, lunch, and dinner on. Martin is in his childhood home.

"There you go, sweetie. Nice and fluffy, just like you like it," says a woman as she sets an omelette in front of Martin.

"Mom? Is that you?" Martin can't believe his eyes. He hasn't seen his mom in decades. He knew that he missed her, but this overwhelming feeling of joy com-bined with grief stuns him. At that moment his dad walks into the kitchen.

"I tell ya, son, it really is great having you here. Your mom and I love it when you pay us a visit."

"But, this . . . this is impossible. You're . . . Both of you are . . ."

Mom pours Martin some more coffee. "Maybe you'd like some more coffee, dear. You don't seem quite awake yet."

"And . . . Dad? You . . . you look great."

"Do I?" Dad inquires, confused by the compliment. "Well, thanks, son. Nice of you to notice." Then he lets out that deep belly laugh that Martin has missed all of his adult life. Transfixed by the sight of his parents, Martin stares at them as Mom and Dad share a concerned look. What does this mean? Has he traveled back in time? Are they visiting him in a dream or was the accident a dream? Are they ghosts? Each thought seems crazier than the last. *Am I dead and they're greeting me?* Martin wonders, perplexed.

Martin snatches the morning newspaper out of his father's hands. "Hey! I was just about to hand the comics over to you. Where are your manners?"

Martin searches frantically for the date on the paper. Today's date is . . . *today's date.* "What?!" Martin blurts out.

"What?" Dad asks, unsure.

Martin looks up from the paper, then back to it.

"It's today . . ." He points to the date on the paper. "But you . . ." He looks back at his mother and father, his mouth is open but he's incapable of forming a coherent sentence.

"Sweetie, maybe you'd like to lie down," Mom suggests.

Martin looks at the date again. He hasn't found himself back in time after all. He's in the here and now, but in *this* here and now, his parents are alive and well. "This is impossible. How can this be?"

"A little nap might do you some good, son." Dad says.

"But . . . Christmas, 1984, the Samuels' party . . . it was raining . . ."

"What are you going on about now?" Dad asks.

Mom remembers. "Oh, yes, the Samuels, they had a big party that year, remember? *The party of the century,* they kept telling us."

"Oh, right, right, the Samuels. Such braggarts," Dad adds.

"But we didn't go, dear. You had the flu something awful," Mom reminds Martin.

"I was sick?" Martin asks.

"Oh, sure, I remember now. Real bad flu. Never seen you like that," Dad says.

"But why are you thinking of that now? Are you not feeling well, sweetie?" Mom asks feeling his forehead.

Martin struggles to remember this version of the past that his parents are telling him about, but he can't because that's not what happened. *It couldn't be.* He thinks. Or else they'd still be alive. A dog's barking interrupts his thoughts.

"You didn't go to the party?" Martin asks his parents.

"No, of course not. You were sick," Mom says.

Overwhelmed with emotion, Martin bounces up and pulls his parents together for a group hug. His parents are surprised but go along with this display of affection from their only son.

"You didn't go! That's awesome!" Martin says.

"Not really. As I recall you were puking your guts out," Dad says.

The dog's barking grows louder.

"Did you get a dog?" Martin asks.

"You know your mom's allergic."

"Where's that barking coming from? It sounds like it's right here."

"I don't hear anything, dear," Mom says.

Martin runs to the window. "How can you not hear that? It's getting louder." He covers his ears.

Dad whispers to Mom, "Maybe we should call Dr. Charles."

The barking grows uncomfortably loud for Martin. He screams, *"Stop barking!"*

He closes his eyes and then POP, he's off zipping through the skies.

He looks down and notices that an identical copy of him is still down below in his parent's kitchen. He envies that other version of himself because he gets to spend more time with them. They really were . . . are . . . great parents. For the first time Martin feels lucky. Lucky to have had them.

*****

Finally Martin arrives back in the sunflower fields. Professor, the dog, sits on his lap and lets out one last bark, then licks Martin's face.

Martin takes a deep breath. He's happy to see this dog, his dog. But just as he settles into this space he hears in the not-too-far-away distance a young boy's voice yelling, "I HAVE TO MAKE A POOP!" And just like that he's zoomed away again. This time the traveling all happens in warp speed, pedal to the metal, cheeks flapping in the wind.

Martin is back in the passenger seat of Pamela's car with their bratty kids. "Oh, God no. Not this one again." It would appear that Pamela has not stopped screaming since the last time he was here.

"Are you listening to me? You never listen! I'm going to take a spa vacation and I might never come back! How do you like them apples?"

Apples? Martin remembers making applesauce in a country *cucina*. He realizes he's thinking in Italian. He remembers briefly dreaming in Pig Latin in the third grade but after that, English was the only language to make an appearance in his subconscious mind. Pamela is still talking loudly and nonstop and the kids are still whining. Martin drowns out the sounds by singing his favorite Italian song. He didn't realize that he had a favorite Italian song but here it is running through his head again.

He closes his eyes as he sings, *sono un italiano*. He makes the decision to stop fighting all of this. He's going to go along for the ride, wherever it takes him. He continues to sing with his eyes shut. Soon, the sensation of being whooshed away takes him once again but this time there's no POP or abruptness. This time it feels gentle, like an ocean wave that collects him and allows him to gently ride the top of it until he's safely delivered to shore.

The shore being - *La Tua Casa*, on a sofa, with Abby caressing his face as he sleepily sings the last refrain . . .

sono un italiano
un italiano vero.

"You should really cut a record," Abby says.

Martin jerks up. "Abby?" He grabs his head as if to physically stop it from spinning.

"Shhh. Lie back down. I think you still need to rest."

"Why? What happened?"

"You heard a phone ring and then you went looking for it. Next thing I know you were passed out on the sofa."

"How long have I been sleeping?"

"Just a couple of hours."

"So, then . . . I'm back? I'm here? I'm really here?" Martin jumps off the sofa and excitedly takes it all in. He touches everything. The antique lamp on the huge, heavy mahogany coffee table. The Arte D'Italia decorative bowls near the fireplace, the Assisi embroidered curtains. Everything looks exceptionally beautiful to him. Especially Abby. Even when her face is looking at him with that mixture of amusement and perplexity. He takes that face into his hands and kisses her mouth.

"I am so happy to be here."

Abby laughs. "Well, I'm also glad you could make it."

"I love this house!" Martin exclaims.

"Good to know," Abby says.

Their dog comes bouncing in, jumping on Martin. Martin swoops him into his arms and allows Professor to lick his face.

"And I love this dog! And you, Abby. I love you."

Martin, in all his forty years on earth has never heard himself utter those three, little, big words to any woman before, besides to his mother as a child. The words echo in his mind, making him feel giddy.

Abby takes Martin's hand and leads him away.

"Where are we going?" Martin asks.

"There's a bedroom you might also love." Abby smiles as she leads him into the bedroom and quietly shuts the door behind them. She playfully pushes Martin unto the bed, then climbs on top of him and seductively removes her blouse. Martin knows what to do, this ain't his first rodeo, but he's caught off guard and more smitten than he ever remembers being, which is making him freeze up. But when Abby snaps off her bra with a flair and throws it behind her, laughing mischievously, Martin thaws and reaches for Abby's face, pulling her in closely. He kisses her deeply and silently prays that this moment won't be the last of its kind. They make love on their grande cherry oak four-poster, romance-novel worthy bed. The sun shines on them like a spotlight. Being with Abby is enthralling, passionate and exhilarating. It's easy. It's like breathing.

Heavy breathing.

The wind blows the curtains gently and Martin can hear the bamboo wind chimes in the distance as he turns to Abby and touches her face once again. She takes his hand off of her face and kisses it, her eyes never leaving his.

"I don't know why you've been acting this way . . . but . . . don't ever stop."

"I'll try not to," Martin says as he lies back and tries desperately to never close his eyes again.

HERE, THERE & EVERYWHERE

When Martin opens his eyes he's still smiling. He rolls over to hug Abby, but instead of Abby, it's the book that he's been cuddling.

His apartment, the one he's lived in for the past ten years, seems like a hovel now. Of course, it *is* a mess, but that mess never seemed to bother him much before. In fact he barely noticed. Now it all seems so dark compared to the light he just came back from. It's as if he'd grown accustomed to grey tones, never realizing that a Technicolor life was possible. Now that he's experienced vivid color, he no longer wants to be here, in the grey. This hue won't do. He wants to be there, in Italy, with Abby, enjoying his life. Still, he's not entirely sure that it's even real. But it feels real, so isn't that good enough?

Martin's head is spinning. He quickly gets dressed and drives over to the professor's office. He barges in, hopped up on WTF energy.

"Isn't it fun?" the professor says as if he was expecting Martin.

"It's not fun, it's disturbing! I don't even know what IT is! Is there an hallucinogen on the pages of that book or something? Am I part of some sort of experiment?"

"You do have quite the imagination! You should do something with that," the professor says.

Martin hasn't stopped moving. He paces around the office.

"They're way too real to be dreams. So . . . delusions?" he asks.

"Delusions are beliefs held by individuals with psychotic disorders, which have no basis in reality and are not influenced by facts. Do you have a psychotic disorder?"

"Then I have some sort of special powers?"

"*Delusions of grandeur.* A belief that one has special powers."

"Well, do I?"

"Do you?"

Martin slams his hands down on the professor's desk the way he imagines James Cagney must have done in an old black-and-white movie.

"What. Is. Going. On?"

The professor, tickled by Martin's intensity, takes a long pause to consider if he should tell Martin the whole story just yet. As if reading the professor's mind, Martin demands, "Tell me!"

The professor lets out a big sigh and gestures to the chair. Martin sits in the chair and waits.

"It was a random search," the professor finally says.

"A random search for what exactly?"

"A person. Any person. To prove that anyone can *see,* given the right tools."

"See what? What tools?"

Martin stares at the professor, waiting for an answer. The professor continues, "Why don't you lie down on the sofa there?"

"Why? Are we going to do some sort of therapy session on me?"

"No, I told you that I'm not a therapist. But your mind is open enough now, so I can show you. Lie down, Martin."

Martin sits on the couch, staring at the professor and pointing his index finger. He wags it at the professor as if to say, *I've got my eye on you, so no monkey business.*

"Relax, Martin. Lie down, close your eyes," the professor instructs, his voice now calm and assertive.

Martin doesn't want to close his eyes. That's when the trouble begins. Although, sometimes when he reopens them he sees Abby. He's so confused and doesn't see much point in fighting this right now. He closes his eyes.

The professor continues, "I, too, was very young when I lost my parents. An accident, just like yours . . ."

Martin is about to ask the professor how he knows about his parents, but the thought of speaking now feels too exhausting. He is suddenly very, very tired.

Martin falls asleep and finds himself in a living room. Not a living room he recognizes. He can hear the professor's voice directing him. He feels more like an observer than a participator this time, like a fly on the wall. Like Scrooge looking into his past. Only this isn't Martin's past.

A sad ten-year-old boy sits on a large sofa, engulfed by it.

He's surrounded by adults wearing black. The boy is staring straight ahead, listening to the adults around him. Martin notices that none of the adults address the little boy. They speak as if he isn't even there.

"It's such a shame," says one.

"They were so young," says another.

"Maybe he was drinking," adds another.

The little boy watches as food plates are passed around. Martin doesn't recognize anyone, but he remembers a similar scene when his parents died. He was the same age as this sad boy who is now being swallowed up by the sofa. Martin remembers hearing everything, seeing everything and yet feeling invisible at the same time. He supposes that if he did have a superpower it would be the power of invisibility. But that power doesn't feel very super. Being invisible can get horribly lonely.

A man bends down and offers the little boy a book. Martin can't see the man's face, only his back. The little boy takes the book.

The man says, in an even, friendly voice, "You're going to be okay, Joey. In fact, you already are. And so are your mom and dad." The man walks past Martin, and that's when he sees his face. It's the professor! The little boy looks down and reads the front of the book. It's the same book the professor gave Martin.

"*More than Meets the Eye: Parallel Lives and Out-of-Body Experiences* by Professor Joseph Welles. Joseph Welles? That's *my* name," says the little boy.

Martin realizes that the little boy is the professor at his parents' memorial. He can see it now. He still has the same wide eyes and wild curly hair that he had as a boy.

The young Professor Joey takes the book and runs upstairs to his room. Martin follows him, in this vision, unnoticed.

Joey hops up on his bed and looks at the cover of the book. "Cool."

He opens up the book and begins to read, eventually falling asleep with the book resting on his belly.

With his eyes closed, as Joey drifts away, a smile appears on his face.

"Wake up!" the professor says, snapping his fingers.

Martin opens his eyes. He glares at the professor.

"I don't get it. *You* gave *little you* a book that *you* wrote? From . . . what? The future?"

"Time is only an illusion," the professor says.

"I don't know what that means."

"Everything happens at once." The professor beams.

Martin puts his head in his hands. The more frustrated Martin gets, the more excited the professor seems. "You give me a headache!" Martin cries.

The professor grabs Martin's hand and rubs the spongy spot between his thumb and forefinger in a circular motion.

"What the hell are you doing?" Martin asks.

"Getting rid of your headache."

Martin thinks about jerking his hand away but doesn't because his headache is vanishing as the professor continues with the hand-rubbing.

"I saw my parents every night after that. All I had to do was close my eyes," the professor says.

"So, you dreamt about your parents and that made you feel better. What does that prove?"

The professor suddenly drops Martin's hand, which bangs into the desk.

"Ow!"

"They aren't *dreams,* Martin. Do you still not see that?"

The professor pouts his way to his computer and types.

"I Googled you," he tells Martin.

"You Googled me?"

"I Googled key words, to find someone like myself, someone I could maybe help," the professor explains.

"What did you Google?"

The professor moves his computer screen so it faces Martin.

Martin reads the words. "*Inquisitive, survivor, male, orphan, creative, lonely.* Seriously? You entered those words into the computer and I just popped up?"

"Hit enter."

Martin hits enter and the top line of the search is a link to an article titled: *Creative, Lonely, Survivor, Telling Other People's Stories.*

"What? What the hell is that?" Martin reads further and remembers. A few years ago a college kid cold-called him, saying he was doing an interview on local filmmakers, and could he ask him a few questions. Martin told him the usual stuff: *stay focused, be prepared, etcetera, etcetera.* The kid was apparently doing a character study, because he describes Martin as a: *Lonely guy who wants to make his own films but continues to shoot other people's films. A lesson in what <u>not</u> to do.*

"That son of a bitch," Martin says. "But, wait, that still doesn't explain how you found me."

"Oh, yes. Well, I'm quite fond of Google. After I read the article, I then searched your name and I found your parents' last name, which led me to a newspaper article about the accident, I suppose since the man in the other car was a well known politician it made the whole thing especially newsworthy. In any case, I thought this was interesting since I had gone through the exact same thing at the exact same age. This fact also proved that you were a survivor, such as myself. I further explored you on your website. Great site by the way."

"So I'm told."

"And then I had the grand idea that if I were to make a documentary about my studies, I could hire you, meet you, and maybe help you."

Martin sits down, taking it all in.

"How many lives have you seen?" asks the professor.

"So, these are past lives then?"

The professor takes a deep breath. "Do you remember the part of the book about the wormholes?"

"Yes. They're . . . portals, to something," Martin says.

"If space can be curved enough, and there is no theo-retical reason why it can't, then maybe . . ."

Martin finishes the sentence, "Then maybe a wormhole could be constructed to shortcut from one side of the universe to the other side?"

"Making it possible to visit our parallel lives." The professor smiles.

Martin sinks back into his chair. "Holy crap."

"Holy crap indeed!"

"You saw your parents, just like I did," Martin realizes.

"In one life, your parents never went to that party." The professor says.

"I had the flu. They stayed home with me."

"Which prevented them from being on the road that night!" The professor exclaims.

It's all coming together for Martin. In one life his parents are alive and well. In another he married the girl he dated in high school and had three terrible children with her. In yet another . . . that one that feels so far away and yet the closest of them all . . . he's in Italy. With Abby.

As if reading Martin's mind, the professor says, "You know her."

"I feel like I do but I've never met her before."

"Not in *this* version of your life."

"So are there more?"

"There are as many lives as there are thoughts."

"What does that mean?"

"Every time you've ever had a substantial, possibly life-changing thought in this lifetime, part of your sub-conscious broke off and turned that *thought* into a *reality*. Every decision you've ever made, all *possible* outcomes actually exist in parallel universes."

"That's crazy."

"I know."

"But if I'm there, am I also here?"

"*'Here, There, and Everywhere.'*"

"What?"

"The Beatles song. It's one of my favorites."

"Please try to stay on track, Professor."

"Right. Well you see, parallel realities coexist, and occasionally, rarely, they can overlap. Like now."

Martin takes a moment to let this sink in.

"So, how do I get back to her?" he finally asks the professor.

"I suppose the same way you got there to begin with."

"Can I stay there?"

"Is *here* so terrible?"

"Yes."

"Well, I don't have all of the answers, my boy. But I do believe you can only truly control the life that you are most aware of. Be here now. It's all very Zen. Why not just enjoy the ride? Treat this time with Abby as a vaca-tion of sorts."

But Martin doesn't want a vacation. He wants to relo-
cate.

Permanently.

"I will have an out-of-body experience.

I will have an out-of-body experience. I will have . . ."

POP!

Martin's body vibrates violently. Martin's spirit detaches from his body. Martin's spirit looks back at his physical body which is still lying down in bed, sleeping. Martin, once again, telepathically speaks down to his body.

"Don't wait up for me."

His spirit self takes off through the ceiling.

Martin is suddenly standing on top of a burning building in full fireman gear. He's a firefighter fighting a fire. He's confused, and not sure what to do about it. If these are his parallel lives shouldn't he be better at doing whatever it is he's supposed to be doing in them?

He notices a fellow firefighter hosing down the fire. It's Rick! Rick gives Martin a thumbs-up. Martin smiles and then closes his eyes firmly.

POP!

He opens his eyes and finds himself on a baseball field. He's a baseball player. A fly ball is coming his way. He lifts his mitt up to catch the incoming ball . . .

POP!

Martin is now in a hospital bed. He feels odd. More emotional and smarter. He's not sure why until he looks down and notices his C-cups. He's a *she*. The nurse brings him his newborn baby. The baby latches on to Martin's breast.

"I want to go home!"

He slams back into his body in his bed at his apartment. He sits up and frantically checks his chest for breasts. He finds none.

Good. That's good.

Martin throws himself back down, exhausted. He thinks about sleeping, but reconsiders. He decides that he should keep his eyes open until he can figure out the whole parallel-life travel thing. Research. That's what he needs to do.

And he needs to come up with some answers soon before Abby completely forgets about him.

WEIRD

Martin has stayed up all night and looks like a man who has stayed up all night. His television is playing the final cut of the quantum physics documentary he shot and his living room is cluttered with books.

Parallel Worlds: A Journey Through Creation, Higher Dimensions, and the Future of the Cosmos by Michio Kaku.

The Great Beyond: Higher Dimensions, Parallel Universes and the Extraordinary Search for a Theory of Everything by Paul Halpern.

OTHERWORLD: Historical Evidence of Parallel Universes by Steve Peek.

Martin paces his apartment, reading passages to himself, eating junk food, searching the internet. Before this moment Martin was content to just fall asleep in front of the TV and dull dreams in greyscale, but now, now . . . Now he's a man obsessed with finding the truth. His thoughts energize him. *What if all of us were constantly bobbing in and out of our lives, wouldn't that get confusing? And why isn't everyone talking about this?*

The professor told him that this was a fluke, a glitch, that it rarely happens. The book helps open the portal for some, but not for everyone. In fact, the professor has only known it to work with children who have suffered a loss. It could be that in some ways Martin is still partly that child who lost his parents so many years ago.

The professor had also told Martin that people were not supposed to remember all the lives at the same time. We're meant to experience each life as it comes, and not remember them simultaneously. Otherwise, if people remembered, they'd go around comparing which life they liked best. But that's not the point of parallel travel. The point is to see how vast the multiverse is, and how all things are possible, and all things are connected. The point is to make the life you are conscious of the best that it can be.

But for Martin, if Abby does not come to him, to this life that he seems to occupy the most, then he must go there, to her. He could live a life in another country, learn another language and be a gracious host even though he's spent a lifetime hating travel, other languages and other people. He could do it if it meant doing it alongside Abby.

Martin turns up the sound on the television. Dr. Lee, one of the quantum physicists in the documentary, is excitedly explaining it all.

"Wouldn't it be amazing if we could, even if just temporarily, witness our other selves? It happens! Whenever we have a thought, a plan, an idea . . . a portion of our "spiritual self" splits off and creates a parallel universe. It hasn't happened to me yet but if it does, I'll bet it would feel like a dream."

Martin begins to put the pieces together. When he'd thought about marrying Pamela, back in the tenth grade, for that nano-second, in one life it actually happened. When he was a kid and told his mom that he was going to be a firefighter and a professional baseball player, he became both of those things somewhere. When he was joking around with his friends in college and said that he didn't think being a woman would be all that tough, well, there ya go, he's breastfeeding a freakin' baby somewhere!

And when his class took that European trip and he declined because of his disdain, or more likely fear, of travel, he did think that maybe Italy would be a cool place to visit.

Still, what good is any of it if he can't control it? A life that you can control, *stay in,* and continue to enjoy is what he wants. Not that Martin feels like he was ever in control in his life, but this recent chain of events just makes that point more evident. Martin thinks, *It's all too strange.*

As if doing the telepathic mind-reading thing, Dr. Lee is back on the television.

"Sure, it's strange. But I've never known a thing worth knowing to be anything but."

NORMAL

"Show me how to get back. I want Abby. That life, with her. I want that." Martin bursts into the professor's office like a bottle rocket, catching the professor dressing his Einstein bust in a Dr. Seuss hat.

"You have that," the professor says, not looking up from Einstein's head.

"I want it *here*. Where I live permanently, without all the buzzing, vibrating, flying, and the who-the-hell-knows where I'm going to be next stuff. I will gladly end this life and trade it for that one!"

"It's just a different version. No better or worse. Just different."

"How can you say that? This version sucks!"

"Does it have to?"

"You're not being much help, you know that?"

"Each possible, probable physical potential for you is happening right now in another universe. I assure you that before this glitch, those lives felt as real to you there as this one does to you here. And once the portal closes, everything will be back to normal."

But Martin doesn't want normal. Not anymore. He remembers reading about a guy who lost his high-paying job when the economy crashed, and he described what it felt like the first time he flew coach. He'd wished that he never flew first class, so he'd have nothing to compare it with. At the time Martin thought this guy was a real putz to be worrying about the loss of first class, but now that Martin has experienced, albeit briefly, a life with love, with laughter, with beauty . . . a first-class kind of life, he can't bear the one he's currently living. He can no longer fly this coach life.

"This is bullshit!" Martin yells.

"This is exactly why we're not meant to know of the others. An occasional dream-like sense is one thing, but to really experience our other lives, we can't help but choose favorites. I knew the portal was opening because it happened to me. I knew the book would get you there. I thought you would take comfort in the experience. I thought you could handle it. I see I made a mistake."

It doesn't feel like a mistake to Martin. It feels important. He doesn't want the conversation to end. He wants answers.

"Why do I always look like me? Even when I had boobs, the rest of me looked like me."

"We take on forms that are most familiar to us. Others might see you differently though," the professor says. "Remember the old TV show, *Quantum Leap?*"

"Yeah."

"Sam always looked like Sam to us, but when he saw his reflection, he saw himself the way others saw him."

Great. I'm living the plot of a TV show from the nineties.

"But it's difficult to ever really see ourselves as others do, so it's tough to say."

Martin is no closer to knowing anything now than he was before the book, the documentary, and this talk.

He stares at the professor. "We have a dog."

"I'm pretty sure you can get a dog in this life as well."

"His name is Professor."

"I'm flattered."

"Why would I do that? Was I sending myself a signal or something?"

"Sometimes wires get crossed. What happens in one life seeps over a bit into the other. Have you ever experienced déjà vu?"

"Sure."

"Sometimes wires get crossed. What happens in one life seeps over a bit into the other. Have you ever experienced déjà vu?"

"You just asked me that."

The professor cracks himself up. Don't you just love a little metaphysical humor?

Martin can't find the funny right now. He just glares at the professor.

"Okay, not your thing. So, how about the feeling that you know someone from before, even though you've just met?" the professor asks.

"Sure, I've felt that before."

"All of that is because you *have* met them and you *have* been there before. Maybe even simultaneously."

Martin puts his head in his hands again, feeling exhausted.

"Look, I'm sure this is just a temporary opening and it'll close soon enough. In the end, you might have fleeting memories, but that's all. In the meantime, enjoy this peek into the mysterious." The professor giggles a little as he leans back in his chair and pretend puffs on his prop pipe.

Martin considers beating him over the head with the Einstein bust.

RICK

Martin and Rick are sitting at a table at their favorite diner, Zane's. Zane's is not a trendy diner where the cool kids go. Hollywood hipsters never find themselves there after a night of tomfoolery. Zane's isn't so much an old-fashioned diner as it is an *old* diner. The paint on the walls is peeling and the booths are not afraid to boast a hefty amount of duct tape in order to keep them together. Old timers frequent the place to read the newspaper from start to finish at a pace that indicates that they have no place to go. At least not urgently. Still, the food is passable, and the coffee is better than anything Martin ever makes at home. Bottom line, Zane's ain't great, which is exactly why it's Martin's favorite place to eat.

Rick merely pretends to tolerate it at Zane's because Martin likes it so much. The lifelong pals worked together for the first time nine years ago on a reality TV show where contestants ate bugs and bungee jumped off of high-rises to win big money. They liked working together so they continue to do so. They both had big dreams of being filmmakers, but managed to merely obtain work as camera operators on reality shows. Martin was always low-key in his aspirations. He behaved as if his desires never had the possibility of actually being fullfilled so he didn't spend much energy wanting them. Still, Rick suspected that his friend had many dreams that were left unexpressed.

When Rick met his wife, Martin said that he was happy for him but Rick sensed Martin's sadness begin to grow. Still, they soon became a mini-production team getting work fairly consistently, but with Rick's new growing family, Martin often felt like an outsider. Rick would love it if he could find a nice woman for his buddy, or get him to reunite with his sister, or talk about his feelings with a shrink. But Rick was never sure what Martin really needed. After Martin tells him the entire story, he's even less sure.

"You need a vacation," Rick says.

"That's it? I tell you that I'm visiting my parallel lives and all you have to say is 'you need a vacation'?"

"Somewhere sunny. The vitamin D will be good for you. And rest, a lot of rest."

"No! No more resting! Resting leads to sleeping and that's when my subconscious slips into the portal, travels through a wormhole, and POP! I'm somewhere else."

"Your other life?"

"Lives." Martin tells him. "My other *lives.* We have many of them. It's wild."

"I'll bet."

Martin takes another sip of his coffee. "Man, the coffee here is great."

"Sure, compared to the crap you usually drink."

"No, I think I know this brand."

"Since when do you know coffee? You've been drinking no-label instant since the day I met you."

"*Lily*. Very popular in Italy."

"Oh, right, I forgot, you're a world-dream-traveler now."

"You were there again."

"Oh, yeah?"

"This time you were fighting a fire with me."

"I was a fireman?"

"We both were. Except I couldn't remember what to do, but you had it under control. Didn't you tell me you wanted to be a firefighter when you were a kid?"

"Yeah," Rick says, enjoying the memory. But then he thinks, *Is that really a big deal?* Lots of little boys want to be firemen. Martin's just dreaming about common youthful fantasies.

"It's there. Within reach." Martin stretches out his arm and grasps the air with his hand.

"What is?"

"Everything we've ever wanted."

Rick gets up to leave.

"Wait, you're leaving?" Martin asks.

"You're kinda freakin' me out, buddy," Rick says.

"You were the one who was always into this stuff. Didn't you always say, 'There are more things in Heaven and Earth that are dreamt of in our philosophy'?"

"Actually Shakespeare said that."

"Well you certainly repeated it a lot."

Martin does have a point. We usually don't go around quoting things that aren't aligned with our own beliefs.

Rick sits back down. "Did the professor say *why* he thinks this is happening to you?"

"He wanted it to happen. It's his book. He wants it to be a valuable tool available for those who are interested in exploring other dimensions. I'm the first adult it's worked on. Apparently children are more open to this stuff."

"All of this because of a book?" Rick asks.

"The professor dedicated his life to this stuff. The book, his book, the words are powerful, they get into your subconscious and then your subconscious spends time proving the theories true."

"Subconsciously?"

"I guess. I mean, it's your subconscious, so how else?"

"Right."

"Words can be powerful. It makes sense. Sort of."

The waitress approaches to pour more coffee for the guys. She smiles at Martin.

"Can I ask you a question?" Martin asks the waitress.

"Martin, *don't*," says Rick.

"Martin, *do*," flirts the waitress.

Rick leans back and puts his hands up in the air as if to ask for some assistance from above.

Martin asks the waitress, "If you met a better version of yourself, living a happier life with a person you were madly in love with, wouldn't you find a way to live there permanently?"

The waitress looks around the mostly empty diner. There's a homeless guy in the corner coughing up some phlegm.

"What? And leave all of this?"

"This coffee we're drinking. It's Lily brand from Italy, right?"

"Please excuse my friend, he's not feeling too well," Rick says.

"Wow. Very impressive." The waitress says to Martin. "The owner is obsessed with that coffee. It costs more than all the others and it's the only coffee he'll have in the place. The girls and I are always kidding him 'cause he cares more about the coffee than the food. Clearly."

The waitress adds before walking away, "If you need anything else just holler."

Martin smiles smugly at Rick.

"Look, even if this was . . . actually happening . . ."

"It *is* actually happening."

"You're not even driving this thing!"

"No. Not yet. But maybe there's a way. Will you help me?"

"Look, just because I have a passing interest in metaphysics and I enjoy the occasional quantum physics discussion, doesn't mean I know anything about anything. I don't think I'd be much help."

Lately, Martin has a way of hearing the exact opposite of what people say.

"Great! We can start tomorrow. I don't think I'll be sleeping much tonight. Gather all the info you can find on the web about this stuff and email me."

Martin takes one last swig of his coffee and happily walks out of the diner. This is the most enthused he's been in a long time. The waitress comes back to the table and pours more coffee for Rick.

"You know, your friend has been coming here for years and this is the first time he's ever spoken to me."

"Yeah, he suddenly has a lot to say."

BE HERE NOW

If sleeping can get Martin there, to all the 'theres' there, then he supposes he could take a sleeping pill and travel at any time. Although he's afraid a pill might be too strong and keep him trapped somewhere, like with Pamela, God forbid. So Martin Yelps a few local meditation classes, to try a drug-free form of relaxation.

Yoga, meditation and any and all spiritual foo-foo has never been Martin's cup of tea. Tea has never been Martin's cup of tea. He doesn't like believing in things that he can't see with his eyes. Of course, that was all before he started flying around the planet and morphing into his other selves. So, yes, Martin would say that he's had a slight change of heart. That's why sitting here now in this yoga studio doesn't feel all that out of the ordinary. He especially likes the name of the studio, *Be Here Now*. The professor just used that expression on him. Also, he finds it ironic, considering that he thinks he *is* being here now, but in truth, he's being many places now. He wonders if the other students, here now, knows what he knows.

The teacher, a skinny, cheerful woman with a blissed-out expression, speaks in hushed, calm tones.

"With each breath you let go even more . . . in through the nose, out through the mouth . . . you are about to embark on a journey . . ."

She has no idea, Martin thinks.

"That's right . . ." the teacher continues. "With each breath we are letting go of all earthly attachments. With each breath we go deeper into the spirit . . . our truth . . . peace and tranquility . . ."

POP!

Martin is in the cockpit of a small plane. He's flying the plane. Only now he is very aware that he has just popped into this life and can't seem to remember how to fly. The plane begins to take a nosedive.

"NOOOOOO!" screams Martin. In the midst of his panic he looks to his right and is shocked to see his sister co-piloting the plane.

"Elizabeth?"

"Don't worry, we'll be okay . . . Stay calm . . . I got it!" she says as she takes over. She rights the plane and gives Martin a thumbs-up.

"I'm sorry I've been such a bad brother . . ."

"Sir?" Elizabeth asks, confused. "What are you talking about?"

Martin thinks about telling her everything. Whomever this version of her is might understand. It's possible.

Martin has learned that all things are possible. He opens his mouth to speak, but before he can get a word out . . .

POP!

Martin is lying down on a bench with the sun on his face. He smiles, feeling like this could be just outside his beautiful B&B and Abby could be nearby.

"Abby?" he says as he sits up to discover that he was lying down on a cement bench, and the smell in the air is not of figs and jasmine but of man-sweat and tar. Martin's eyes meet Bubba's. Bubba is a six-foot-six monster of a man with skull tattoos running up his neck and not stopping at the face but continuing into a snake tattoo that circles his left cheek.

"What the . . ." Martin looks around him. There's a tall chain-link fence and a lot of cement. He's in a cold, ugly enclosure of some sort.

Oh, shit, Martin thinks, *I'm in a prison yard!* He desperately tries to remember what could've brought him here. He remembers that he had a friend, back when he was in his early twenties, who wanted him to carry a package to his family in Mexico. The friend assured Martin that it wasn't anything illegal, but that he couldn't get away because he had a big test coming up. He offered Martin a great hotel on the beach and cash. He told Martin he could bring a friend and they'd have the time of their lives. Martin considered it for a moment but then remembered how much he hated traveling so he stayed put. He found out later that the guy who went in his place was arrested for drug smuggling. Maybe, in one life, *Martin* was the one who delivered that package.

This isn't good, Martin thinks as Bubba leans in, looking like he's about to settle some sort of disagreement. Martin closes his eyes.

POP!

Martin, exhausted, now lies on his back in the sunflower field. "Abby," he whispers to himself. Then, "Abby!" he yells at the top of his lungs.

"Martin? Where are you?"

Martin gets up quickly and pushes the tall sunflowers aside, desperate to see Abby, who is running towards him.

"Are you okay? What's the matter?" she asks.

Martin kisses her. "Nothing. Everything's perfect now." Martin says in between kisses.

Abby laughs. "What's gotten into you? You keep wandering off and then when I find you again you act like . . . this."

"Just meditating in the sunflower fields."

"Why were you screaming for me like that?"

"I missed you." He plants more kisses on her.

Abby playfully pushes him away. "You're a weirdo." Then she pulls him close again. "But you're my weirdo."

The dog joins them, barking enthusiastically.

"Hey, Professor." Martin picks up the dog and hugs him. "I missed you too."

"Okay, weirdo, let's get ready. We're leaving in five."

"Where are we going?" Martin asks.

"The same place we go every Friday," Abby says. "Stefano cleaned up the *biciclette* for us. They're out front. Meet you there!" Abby runs off and Professor wiggles out of Martin's arms to follow her.

"Biciclette?"

BIKE RIDE

Martin and Abby ride their bicycles in the quaint little town of Cingoli, which, apparently, they do every Friday to pick up groceries for a big Friday-night dinner. After three kilometers they stop to pick up a bottle of wine. After another two, they stop to get freshly baked bread. They have a little more to go for the fresh fruit and vegetables.

How fun!

How European!

How exhausting!

Martin has not participated in any form of exercise for most of his adult life. He took to sloth and laziness quite well, and with no one around to tell him to be otherwise, he never became otherwise. He doesn't understand why he doesn't have a better body in *this* version of himself, but assumes it's part of the wires-crossing thing.

Excited, because this is the longest he's been able to stay with Abby so far, he tries desperately to keep up. But, as beautiful as the scenery is, as beautiful as Abby is, Martin can't keep up. He's out of breath, struggling to pedal and Abby and the dog, who's riding in the basket, are way ahead of him.

"Are you okay back there?" Abby yells back at him.

"Yes! I'm great!" Martin lies.

Abby pulls her bike off to the side and takes Professor out of the basket. They sit under an apple tree on the side of the road and wait for Martin to catch up. He looks like the same Martin she married, but he certainly has been acting oddly. She suspects something's up, but she doesn't know what.

Martin finally arrives and gets off his bike. He waddles over to Abby and Professor and plops himself onto the blanket that Abby has set out. Abby pulls out a bottle of wine from her backpack.

"Where did that come from?" Martin asks. Abby opens the bottle and pours two glasses into little plastic wine cups.

"You know I always think of everything," Abby says, handing him a glass.

"It's Rosso Conero. Your favorite," she adds.

Martin drinks the wine, happy to be doing anything but riding. He stares at Abby like a smitten schoolboy.

"Stop it," Abby says. "You're being too weird, even for you. And what's with the heavy breathing? Are you sick?"

"No, I'm just . . . a little out of shape, I guess."

"Since when?"

Martin wants her to know everything. Everything there is to know about him, *the real him,* whomever that is. He wants her to know that he wants to stay. He wants to tell her that this has been a crazy trip and the only good thing to come from it is her. The only good thing to come from his life, any of his lives, is her. How can he tell her in a way that will make it all sound . . . believable?

"I never want to leave you," he tells her.

"Good to know."

"Does it ever feel like I have?"

"Have what?"

"Left."

"What do you mean?"

"Do I ever seem different to you? Like I'm somewhere else?"

"Lately you've been a little spacey, but I wouldn't say that you're somewhere else. Why? What's this about?"

"If I ever seem like I'm somewhere else just know that I'd rather be here. I'd always rather be here."

"Got it. Now tell me what the hell is going on."

Martin knows this is his chance. His chance to have a true partner in all of this craziness. Once Abby knows, maybe she can help him figure it all out.

"Can I tell you anything?" he asks.

"You know you can," she assures him.

Martin takes a deep breath and then pours a full glass of the Rosso Conero for Abby. He motions for her to drink.

"You're gonna need that."

ALWAYS HERE

Abby is pacing now and drinking the vino straight from the bottle. She can't understand why her husband would make up such a cockamamie story. Why would he feel the need to invent such a ludicrous lie? Is their life together not interesting enough? Is this ideal life that they created here in Italy, after years of careful saving and planning, is it not what he had imagined it would be? She considers that Martin could be having a mid-life crisis. She wonders why he couldn't just have an affair like a normal man? At least an affair would be something solid. It would be something happening in the real world that she could somehow find a way to react to. She could leave him or forgive him. But *this* . . . this is . . . *what is this?*

"Why would you make up such an insane story like that?"

"Exactly! I wouldn't!"

"Are you unhappy here?"

"Unhappy? Are you nuts? You're the best thing that's ever happened to me!"

"This doesn't make any sense! You're always *here*!"

"To *you*, yes. To you I'm always here, but it doesn't feel like that to me."

"I don't understand."

"Most of us only experience one life at a time. That's how it's supposed to be. Something happened that has allowed me to spend some time in my other ones. But still, the predominant life, the one I've grown the most accustomed to, that's the one I keep being pulled back to. That's the guy I feel that I am in all my lives, regardless of how others see me. But it's different here. Here, with you, I'm me but just . . . so much better."

Abby considers this. What he's saying makes no rational sense, but at least it doesn't indicate that he'd rather be anywhere but here.

"So then what does it feel like when you're not here?" She snaps.

"When I'm not here, in my main life I'm . . . I don't know . . . Just going through the motions. It's horrible. In my main life I drink crappy instant coffee, I live in a small, dark apartment, I hardly take care of myself and I only have one friend. I'm kind of . . . pathetic."

"Why?" Abby asks, still annoyed.

"I told you, the professor gave me a book and . . ."

"No, not *how*. *Why*. Why do you live that way?"

Martin takes a moment to consider this question. He has no idea how to answer it. Has anyone ever asked him that? Rick may have skirted around the idea that Martin could visit a gym once in a while. Susan has gently suggested he get some new clothes and maybe "get out a little." His sister calls and leaves messages even though he never calls back. Sure, he supposes that people have tried to reach out and, in their way, ask him that question, but never this directly.

"I don't know," Martin answers. Which of course is no answer at all.

Abby shakes her head from side to side. After a moment she sighs, "It's too crazy."

"I know," Martin agrees.

"You've never made up stories before. You've never lied to me."

"And I'm not now and I never will."

Abby sits back down and Professor curls up on her lap.

"Do you have another wife?" she asks him.

"No. I have nothing."

"How do I know that's true? I can't see you when you're not here because I always think you *are* here!"

"I know it's confusing . . ."

"No! I'm not confused. *You* are. This is insanity!"

Abby abruptly gets up and hops on her bike.

"Where are you going?" Martin yells after her. Professor barks.

"I need to think!" she yells without looking back.

Professor chases after her and runs by her side as she rides away.

"Oh! And our dog is named after a real Professor!" Martin yells.

"Abby!" He yells after her once more. Frustrated, Martin lies down on the grass and plucks a sunflower from the ground. He stares at it for a moment and then crumbles it. He tosses it aside and screams up to the heavens, "Abby!"

POP!

Martin's eyes are still shut and he's still screaming "Abby!" when he finds himself seated cross-legged in his meditation class. He opens his eyes and looks around to a class full of yogis staring at him.

"Tourette's," he explains to the onlookers. The teacher puts her hand to her heart. "Oh, you poor thing."

The class nods in compassionate agreement.

RESEARCH

Martin is at his computer feeling restless and annoyed, devouring a bag of Cheetos. He told Abby the truth, so why doesn't he feel better? He thought the truth would heal. He thought the truth shall set him free. Not yet, apparently. It would appear he has some more work to do.

An instant message pops up from Rick on Martin's screen.

Hey, buddy. I thought you might like these sites I found for you. Click Here.

Martin clicks and finds himself at iSeeSpirits.com

A page full of ghostly creatures and blogs from people who are obsessed with spirits.

You could be sharing a bed with the dearly departed.

"You're a riot, Rick." Martin tells the computer screen.

Another message from Rick: *Or maybe you'd prefer this one.*

Martin clicks on the next link and the page WeAreNotAlone.com comes up.

They are living among us . . . your best friend could actually be an alien.

Martin remembers that Rick does have freakishly close-set eyes. Could be.

Rick again: *And last but not least – Shapeshifters.com*

Martin continues to go along with Rick and his mockery by clicking this link as well. ***I've been everything from an orangutan to the president of the United States. You can shape-shift too if you follow these three easy steps.***

Rick sends a laughing face emoticon. Martin responds with a delightful middle finger emoticon.

Martin looks down on the keyboard and realizes that it's covered in orange Cheeto dust. He stares at the powder. He licks a finger and dips it on the keyboard, and then licks the finger again.

He soon begins to feel nauseous. Must be all of that zooming around from life to life stuff. He goes to the bathroom and stares at his reflection in the mirror. He's a tubby, dirty mess. He opens the cabinet, reaches for the Pepto Bismol and takes a swig, leaving a pink Pepto mustache on his face. He takes in his reflection. Orange Cheeto dust on his fingers and t-shirt, and pink Pepto cream on his face.

Gross yet colorful, he thinks. Martin stares at the shower as if waiting for it to invite him in. It doesn't. So, instead of freshening up, he goes to bed.

He lies on his side watching the opened book on the nightstand. He knows what he's supposed to say by heart now. He knows how to take a deep, cleansing breath and he knows that he can probably just fall asleep, and without trying at all, he will zip around to and fro and arrive somewhere. He also knows that he can meditate and "embark on a journey" as his meditation teacher suggested. But when he closes his eyes, when he embarks on his journey, he's never positive where he'll end up, and he knows that he won't stay long. Knowing how perfect it all is with Abby in Staffolo just makes everything else feel like he's slumming it. Still . . . what else is going to do? There's nothing for him here, in L.A., in this life.

He needs to get out.

So . . . get out he will.

Martin takes a deep breath and closes his eyes.

I will now leave my body . . . I will now leave my body . . .

I will now leave my body . . .

POP!

Martin wakes up in a bathtub with Abby. Candles are lit. The *Mia Martini Minuetto* is their soundtrack. They are drinking red wine, facing one another. Martin is overjoyed to be there. Abby stares intensely at him. She thinks that maybe, just maybe, it's all true. What would be his motivation to make up such a story? Since they opened *La Tua Casa*, Martin has been calmer and happier than she's ever seen him. He never gave any indication

111

that he wished he was someplace else. She figures, at least the way he tells it, that the Martin she gets is the best version of him. So that should count for something.

"I should really write all of this stuff down. It would make a great story," Abby says.

Martin studies the naked Abby, unable to form a sentence. He finally manages to speak. "Wow. Just look at you."

"I'm not kidding, Martin. The stuff you told me. If you don't write it down, I will. I've always thought I'd like to try my hand at writing. I like sci-fi and romance. Comedy too. Maybe I'll write a hybrid genre of some sort. Maybe I'd be good at it. You never know, right?"

Martin knows that better than anyone.

"It's true, you never know."

Abby has loved Martin since the day she met him twelve years ago. He was a sad man. A man who wasn't quite sure how the rest of his life was going to pan out. *A man without a plan,* is what her mother had told her. But still, there was something about him. He hadn't totally given up on life, but he was headed in that direction. It's too trite to say that she wanted to save him, it wasn't that. It was that she thought they could save each other. And they did. Abby decides in that moment, there in the tub, if Martin says he's visiting his other lives, then so be it.

He's here now and that's all that matters. Besides, it makes for a good story.

"I believe you," she tells Martin.

Martin leans in for a kiss. They continue kissing as they sink further into the tub. Abby is laughing as they both go under the water, still kissing.

Martin was never much of a bath-taker. He was a shower guy through and through. Truth be told, he didn't much care for showers either. He would hit all the important spots, soap up, rinse and be done with it. Get in. Get out. *Finito.* But in this bath with Abby, under the water, it feels the way it always looked like it should feel in the movies. In the movies, being underwater looks like pure, magical, artful tranquility. He wishes he could hold his breath longer so he could continue to enjoy this tranquility, but soon remembers that he'd rather come back up and enjoy more of the naked Abby.

He comes up from under the bathwater and shakes his head like a puppy coming in from the rain. He waits for Abby to giggle and playfully smack him like she does when she pretends that she's mad at him. But all is quiet.

Not only is all quiet but all is . . .

"CRAP!" Martin pounds his fists on the top of the water upon realizing that this is his water.

In his bathtub.

In his apartment in Los Angeles.

He didn't even know he had a bathtub.

THE MALL

<u>Two Weeks Later</u>

Malls suck. That's the way Martin has always felt. They're full of greedy commerce and pushy people. Normally he would never come within five miles of a mall, but this is where Rick and Susan and the kids are on this particular Sunday. It's an outdoor mall so Martin figures it might not suck so badly. He has no choice, really. He needs someone to talk to, and these are the only someones he's got. For two weeks now Martin hasn't been able to travel to any of his other lives. Not the old ones, and not any of the new ones. For two weeks he hasn't been anywhere but here.

"It's like the portal or whatever just suddenly closed up," Martin tells them for the billionth time.

"Maybe it's better this way, bud," Rick says.

"No, it's not. Don't say that. Abby probably hasn't even noticed. She says that she thinks I'm always there so she wouldn't even be looking for me."

"Look for you how?" Susan asks.

"I don't know. I just feel so alone in this."

"You're not alone, Uncle Martin!" says Jack, pulling on Martin's pant leg.

Martin smiles down at Jack for a brief moment, then continues with his lamenting. "I just can't fucking believe this!"

"Daddy, Uncle Martin said the F-word!" Jerry says.

"You need a time out, mister!" Jack chimes in.

"Martin, do you mind?" Rick says pointing to his kids.

Martin kneels down to get eye-level with Jack and Jerry.

"Listen, guys, I'm sorry, but this is F-word stuff here. I'm talking about everlasting happiness, wormholes and true love, do you understand?

The kids stare blankly at their crazy uncle Martin as they contemplate worms inside of holes. Susan points them towards the mall jungle gym. "Hey, doesn't that look fun? Off you go."

Jack and Jerry run off to play on the swings. The adults find a nearby bench and have a seat. They're all silent for a few moments.

Rick is thinking that he's glad Martin's dreams have stopped, because it was getting out of hand.

Martin is thinking that he's lonely, misunderstood and a little bonkers.

Susan is thinking that something good could come of this experience.

"Martin, can I ask you something?" asks Susan.

"Sure."

"What if this Abby of yours was here? Would she be into you?"

"What do you mean?"

"Jeez, Susan . . ." says Rick.

"No, go on, Susan, what do you mean?" Martin asks.

"It's just . . . if this amazing woman was actually here right now, do you think she'd be . . . and no offense, I'm just making a point here . . . do you think she'd be drawn to . . . you?"

Martin considers this. He looks down at his Cheeto-stained t-shirt and pot belly then runs a hand through his uncombed hair. How long has he been such a mess?

"Susan, let the guy alone," Rick says.

"No, keep talking," Martin tells Susan.

"I mean, she sounds pretty awesome, from the way you describe her."

"She is. She is awesome," Martin agrees.

"Right. So, in my experience, awesome women are attracted to . . . awesome men."

"Jesus, Susan," Rick gasps.

"Calm down, Rick. Martin knows I love him. Right, Martin?"

"Yeah, sure," Martin says.

"And you know that Rick and I, *we* think you're awesome."

"Yeah, man!" Rick agrees, a little too enthusiastically.

Susan places her hands on Martin's shoulders and looks him directly in the eyes. "But it's not enough that *we* know it. You know?"

They all grow quiet for a bit. Martin thinks about all of the years he's been wandering, doing only what was necessary to survive. Get up, get some work, eat some food, pay some bills, go to sleep and try not to dream of the past.

Losing his parents at such a young age was tragic, but not being able to talk about it made it doubly so. When his grandparents, his mother's parents, raised him and Elizabeth after the accident, they refused to talk about it. Any of it. It was as if remembering their daughter made it all too unbearable. So they didn't talk about her. Ever. This made the anger and loneliness in Martin build into a steel-plate wall with no access in. Elizabeth dealt with the pain in other ways. She had a brief rebellious phase, but once she got over that, she found a way to express her pain through photography, she formed friendships, fell-in-love, started a family, carving out a place for herself in the world. She went to therapy and pleaded with Martin to join her, but he never did. Martin thinks, *I'm forty years old. How much more of my life can be ruled by this one event?* He thinks that maybe, underneath his unkemptness is a good-looking man and underneath his fear is a hopeless romantic who will do anything for love. Even if that includes bettering himself.

Martin smiles wildly, gets up, grabs Susan and plants several kisses all over her face.

"Hey! No man-handling my wife! My baby's in there!"

Martin turns, grabs Rick and proceeds to plant several kisses all over his face as well and then he takes off running.

Rick turns to his wife, "I hope you know what you're doing."

PART TWO

One Week Later

Martin's alarm clock goes off with Bobby Darin's, *Dream Lover*.

Martin, not usually a fan of irony, laughs it off. He closes his eyes and then opens them wide, as if testing the magic that used to be. He reaches his arm out to his left to feel around for a bed partner. No such luck. In this moment he knows that he has a choice to make. He can choose to be miserable here, in this life, without Abby. Or he can do something else entirely.

He stands in front of his closet which is full of jeans and black tees. He rummages through the mess and finds nothing. He looks up and notices that he has one clean, dark blue suit hanging in his closet. It's covered in plastic with a sticky note that says, *weddings and funerals*. He figures that he's the one who made that rule so he can break that rule. He crumples up the sticky note and throws it on the floor. Then he stares at the crumpled note on the floor, picks it up, and tosses it in the trash.

He begins his day the way he imagines people who have their shit together begin their day. He makes his bed, takes a shower and brushes his hair, then puts on his pressed suit before heading into the kitchen. His mind wanders for a moment to Abby, their *cucina* at La Tua Casa, and their cozy warm Sunday mornings together. He, out of habit, reaches for his *Screw This I'm Going Back to Bed* mug and instant coffee but then shakes his head quickly, hoping to remove the memory and the habit. He throws out his angry mug and instant coffee and walks to the hallway closet. In the closet sits a large, wrapped gift. There's a card.

"Hey big bro, hope you're doing well. We'd love to see you sometime. In the meantime, enjoy some <u>real</u> coffee. Merry Christmas. Love, Elizabeth."

Martin opens the box to find a French press and a bag of *Lily* Italian coffee grounds. He's never worked one of those fancy coffee-making devices before but there's no time like the present to figure it out. He finds a spot for it on the kitchen counter and looks at it quizzically for a moment. After reading the instructions Martin attempts to make a real cup of coffee for the very first time. He waits the suggested amount of time and then pushes down the press, making the coffee squirt everywhere in all directions. He had skipped over the word *gently* in "*gently* push down the press." In the past, spilling coffee all over the place would have been the sort of thing that would make Martin want to call it a day. Instead, he carries on.

On the next attempt he uses too much coffee. The press won't push down at all. He uses both hands. The French press goes flying off the counter. *No worries,* Martin says to himself. He pauses for a moment, shocked by the carefree expression that had just passed his lips. He cleans up the mess. On the third attempt, he's smooth, slow and gentle, and at last, he has before him *a real cup 'o Joe.*

Martin sits on his patio, sipping and enjoying his coffee the way he knows he would do if he were with Abby. Martin thinks to himself that this whole "acting as if" thing feels quite good. No wonder it's all the rage in the spiritual circles. He looks down and notices his dying plant. The sight of it propels him up to grab a pitcher of water. Feeling like a man of action feels kind of good. He waters his plant, noticing that some of the leaves still have some green in them. *Hmmm,* He thinks, *maybe it's not too late after all.*

Next, Martin tackles that huge pile of mail on his living room table. The one from the Indie Filmmakers Grant is one he should have opened long ago. He wonders what stopped him. Was he afraid of being denied or was he afraid of being approved? Martin has grown sick and tired of being afraid.

He reads the letter.

It is with great pleasure that we inform you that your grant proposal has been accepted. Please call the phone number at the bottom of this page as soon as possible to set up a meeting to discuss this further. Congratulations!

Well, how about that? Martin thinks. He hasn't had good news in so long, he's not sure what to do about it. What is it most people do when something good happens? Martin turns on the radio. The oldie station is playing Rick James', *Superfreak.* Martin dances around his apartment until he's a sweaty mess. He dances a hip-shaking, booty bouncing, touchdown-making dance. When the song finishes he feels he needs to do more. Maybe something he hasn't done in a long time.

The first twenty minutes on the phone with his sister is mostly spent on Elizabeth's surprise. He finally tells her about the grant.

"It's pretty cool, right?"

"I'm so happy for you. Also, you sound . . . different. Are you okay?" Elizabeth asks.

Martin cradles the phone on his neck as picks away the dead leaves from his plant.

"Yeah, actually. I am," Martin realizes.

"Does that mean we'll see you this Christmas?"

"Oh, I don't know . . . The thing is . . . I could be out of the country this Christmas."

"My brother leaving the country? This I gotta see. Where?"

"Italia," Martin says.

Elizabeth laughs at her brother's choice to use the Italian word instead of the English word.

"Hey, remember when all your friends went on that Italian tour in college? You were the only one who didn't go."

"Yeah, I guess I wasn't ready."

"And now you are?"

"Definitely."

"Well, if you're not traveling the world, your nephew would love to see you. So would your sister."

"Thanks again for the gift," Martin says, changing the subject.

"I don't even remember what we got you. That was ten months ago."

"The coffee thing."

"Oh, right, of course, the coffee thing."

"I love it."

"I'm glad."

Martin stops futzing with the plant and sits down. He's thinking that he should probably break the silence and say goodbye, but it feels so good just to be on the phone with Elizabeth after all of this time that he doesn't want it to end. He feels like he's been such a putz to allow so much time to pass, avoiding the very people who love him.

After a moment Martin says, "I love you, sis."

If Elizabeth is startled by this verbal display of affection from her estranged brother, she doesn't let it appear in her voice.

"I love you too, big bro."

NEW PLAN

<u>One More Week Later</u>

It's been an entire month now senza Abby. This fact would be unbearable if not for Martin's new plan.

The last time Martin ran anywhere it was because he was on fire about the dreams and had to reach Rick quickly but Martin never understood the *desire* to run.

"I'm going for a run," is a freakish phrase Martin has heard Rick utter time and time again. Martin understands running *towards* something in order to get there first, like in a race. But he only understands that in theory. He mostly understands running *away* from something. But not literally. Literal running involves energy, movement, and sweat. But now Martin is determined to lose his floppy belly for the first time in his adult life. Also, there's a rumor going around that exercise makes you think clearer and stimulates the dopamine in your brain, which can make you happy. *Happy* could very well be what Martin is running towards.

Every day for the past two weeks Martin has awoken to music, sang with said music, brushed his hair, shaved, mad and drank real coffee, cleaned and put away the dishes, and gone for a morning run. He's lost six pounds and is shaping up to look like a fairly attractive guy. Maybe even slightly better than fairly.

"Thanks for finally letting me come with you, mystery guy," Rick says as he runs next to Martin.

"I just needed some 'me time,' you know?" Martin says.

Rick laughs. "I never thought you were the running type. Or the 'me time' type."

"Yeah, well, I'm re-writing me."

"Say again?"

"It's up to me what kind of guy I am, right?"

"I guess so. Well, you look good."

"Thanks," Martin says, wiping the sweat from his forehead.

"Why don't you come with us to our Christmas in Hawaii vacation? Susan and the kids would love to have you."

"Elizabeth invited me to her place."

"Are you going?"

"I don't know yet."

Martin suddenly stops. A blonde woman jogs past him. He turns to watch her. He stares at her back for a moment and then breaks out into a sprint towards her.

"Buddy! What are you doing?" Rick yells after him.

Martin catches up to the jogger, grabs her by the shoulder and turns her to face him. "Abby!" he exclaims, thrilled to have found her! Without missing a beat, the woman who is not Abby whips out her pepper spray.

Rick yells from afar, "Mistake! Mistake! Honest mistake!"

The jogger takes her hand off of the trigger.

"Creep," she sneers before taking off again.

Martin, defeated, sits down on the curb and puts his head in his hands. Rick joins him.

"You okay?"

"She's out there. Do you have any idea how frustrating that is? To know that the love of your life is out there, almost within reach, but you can't get back to her, and when you can get back, you can't stay. Do you have any idea what that's like?"

"No, buddy. I don't."

Martin stares at his shoes, noticing that his shoelaces are almost undone. He undoes them all the way and then reties them. He continues to do this, on a loop, which would normally make him feel like a crazy person, but he's just happy to have his mind occupied by something other than who he's missing. Rick watches for a while until he can't take it anymore. He pushes Martin's hands aside and ties Martin's shoes in a double knot. Martin mutters a 'thanks' and sighs deeply.

"At least she's out there, right? I mean, you know that she exists. That's got to count for something." Rick says.

"Does that mean you don't think this is all just a dream anymore? You believe me?"

"For some unexplainable reason, I believe you." Martin puts his arm around his buddy.

"Thanks."

"Don't mention it." After a moment he adds, "Seriously, don't mention it. To anyone."

Martin is lying down on the professor's couch, staring at the ceiling. He silently counts each square tile by twos. He finds this slightly OCD behavior comforting. The professor hasn't taken his eyes off of him. Martin's always aware when people are staring at him and he usually assumes they're thinking the worst.

"You look good. Better. Much better," the professor says as he puffs his pipe and blows smoke rings.

"I thought the pipe was just a prop."

"I felt like taking the relationship further."

"Smoking is a nasty habit."

"So is wallowing."

Martin stops counting the tiles. He sits up.

"What was the point of all of this?" he asks the professor.

"The point to gaining mind-expanding knowledge and experience is just that."

"Just what?"

The professor leans his pipe against the Einstein bust, removes Einstein's scarf and dramatically wraps it around his own neck. "Gaining mind-expanding knowledge and experience."

"Well, it's not enough."

"It's more than enough, Martin, ol' pal! Look at you. You've changed. You've become aware. You're alive with the possibility of it all!"

"I did all of this for her!"

"You did all of what for her?"

"Changed my life, started taking care of myself, you know, got it together."

"Well, it would seem that someone else might also benefit from such a transformation."

"Why even know that this better life exists if I can't live it?"

"You *are* living it, Martin. Trust it."

"I don't even understand it! How can I trust it? Don't you get it? Knowing that I could be so happy was so . . ." Martin struggles to find the right word.

". . . Inspiring?" the professor asks.

"Yeah. Inspiring."

"That's wonderful!" exclaims the professor. "From that inspiring feeling you will attract incredible things into your life. In fact, the great Dr. Lee has a theory . . ."

Martin doesn't want to hear it. He's through with other people's theories. There's no point in seeing "other worlds" or "other possibilities" or any of that crap if he has no control over it. He doesn't give a damn if that stupid wormhole, portal, bubble, string, whatever, ever opens up again. He cuts off the professor before he can launch into another theory.

"No more theories! Except for one. *Mine.* Here's my theory, Professor. My theory is that *this* life, the one I'm experiencing *right now,* in this very moment, is the only one I can actually feel 100% of the time, so it, and only it, should better damn well be the one I focus on!"

Martin storms out of the professor's office, slamming the door behind him.

The professor smiles broadly, "Good theory."

DECEMBER 22ND

<u>One Year Later</u>

Last Christmas Martin Skyped with his sister and nephew promising them that he would see them the following year. At the time he felt as if he was working on something, that something being himself, and he wanted it to be presentable before he unveiled it. A year has passed, and he's not entirely sure if he's worthy of an unveiling just yet.

But he made a decision that day, a year ago in the professor's office, that he would no longer dwell on what he's lost. After all, he never truly had it to begin with. He possessed only pieces of that life with Abby in Italy. How does one hold on to *pieces* of a life? Martin wanted a whole life, so his theory was *-commit to his own life.* He still thinks of Abby, but he no longer remembers his dreams, which is just as well. The longing was too painful to endure.

Today Martin sits in the kitchen of his clean, brightly painted apartment, eating a meal of grilled salmon on a bed of greens he purchased at the farmer's market earlier that day. A beautiful, healthy potted plant sits on the countertop. His daily jogs and healthy eating have taken years off of him. A shiny trophy sits on top of the fridge. On it is engraved: *"My Lives," a film by Martin Henry Stazinski.* Attractive and accomplished, yet still alone. Well, not completely alone. An adorable Jack Russell terrier comes bouncing in and jumps on Martin's lap with a bark.

"Hey, Professor. What's up? Want to go for a run?"

*****

Martin talks with Rick on his Bluetooth while the dog jogs beside him. "Merry Christmas. How's Hawaii?"

"It's great. The kids love it. But even after all of these years, I still find it disturbing to see mall Santas wearing shorts. "

"Kinda creepy."

"Are you still running?" Rick asks.

"Every day."

"Impressive."

"Not really. It's just one foot in front of the other."

"I get how it works. What are you doing for the holidays this year?"

"Not sure yet."

"The invitation still stands if you want to join us for Christmas."

"Thanks, but Hawaii has a dog quarantine and I can't leave Professor on Christmas. He'd be crushed."

"He's a dog. He'd get over it."

"He's very sensitive. And he's also a genius." Professor has stopped running at this point and has begun to lick himself with great intensity.

"Maybe you'll see Elizabeth?"

"Rick, me and Professor are just fine on our own."

"Okay, buddy, okay. Merry Christmas to you both then."

"Thanks. Merry Christmas to you too."

Martin hangs up the phone and nudges Professor with his foot. Professor stops licking and continues to run by Martin's side. They run until nightfall. Martin thinks of *Forrest Gump* and can't remember how that movie ended. He hopes happily.

Run, Martin, Run.

Martin sits in front of his TV wearing a Santa's cap next to Professor who's wearing reindeer antlers. Elizabeth has left several messages inviting them both over, but Martin isn't quite sure he's up to it. This whole bettering-himself business has been exhausting, and he's not sure he can handle the "what-ifs" of a Christmas spent with family.

What if . . . other than his outward appearance, which has greatly improved, they can tell that he still has remnants of the sad, lonely, bitter Martin? *What if* . . . his sister gives him that "poor Martin" look? *What if* his sister looks more like their mom than she did the last time he saw her and he just loses it completely?

It's safer to stay put, Martin thinks to himself as he channel surfs with Professor's chin now resting on his leg.

It's a Wonderful Life plays on the television. It's the scene where George Bailey is thinking about jumping. Martin switches the channel.

When Harry Met Sally: the scene where Harry runs towards Sally to meet her at the New Year's Eve party. He turns off the TV.

"Want to go for a run?" Martin asks Professor. The dog picks up his chin from Martin's leg and then quickly places it back down and closes his eyes.

"Yeah. Me neither."

He turns the TV back on, flipping the channel to QVC. There's a lady getting very excited about an emerald necklace, "Oh my! This is certainly a sensational last-minute gift for that someone special in your life."

Martin turns the TV off again and gets up, knocking the sleeping dog to the ground.

"Sorry, Professor. I need to get out of the house."

*****

Martin and Professor, still wearing their respective festive hats, stare into the window of Zane's. A handful of diners are enjoying their time with one another, reminding Martin that this is what some people do. They enjoy spending time with others. Channeling Babs he sings to himself, *People who need people are the luckiest people in the world.*

Martin watches as a group of women sit at a round table and enjoy one another's company, laughing and carrying on. They probably just came from an office Christmas party. They undoubtedly have tons of inside jokes, and they most likely bond over their mutual disdain for their boss. One of the women wears the same reindeer antlers that Professor wears. Martin finds his ice-breaking line. He looks down at his dog.

"I need to be with humans. Nothing personal."

Professor lies down and stays put as Martin enters the diner and approaches the table of women.

"Good evening, ladies," Martin says, sounding more like *Frasier* than himself. The women laugh.

"Good evening, *gentleman*," mocks the antler-wearing woman.

The women are a bit tipsy, but this doesn't deter Martin.

"You all seem to be having a good time," Martin notices.

"We escaped the office Christmas party," one says.

"Boooooring," adds another.

"Yeah, the nog was weak."

One of the ladies takes out a flask of whiskey and adds it to their egg-nogs. They all raise their egg-nog glasses and clink. "To strong nog!"

Martin addresses the antler-wearing women, "My dog has those too."

She stops laughing and says, "Your *dog*?"

Sensing he's said something wrong Martin begins to ramble, "He looks really cute in it. I mean, so do you. You also look cute. I mean, I think they make them for dogs as well. I got mine at Petco, did you get yours at Petco?"

"No. I did not get mine at Petco." She takes off her antlers and glares at Martin. He walks away from the table with a small, muttered, "Merry Christmas."

Martin looks around the diner to scope out his choices for temporary diner companionship. He sees a father with his toddler son who has cake frosting all over his face. The father notices Martin watching and smiles at him with a nod. That's enough invitation for Martin, he approaches.

"He loves his cupcakes," the father tells Martin.

"I can see that." Martin smiles.

"I love bringing him home all messy. His mother hates it."

Martin stands there, searching his mind for polite conversation.

"How old is he?"

"Twenty months."

"Wow. He's so big."

The father's expression changes from joyous to worried.

"You think so? I mean, maybe a little. It's his mother's fault. She feeds him crap."

Martin can't remember if there ever was a time when he said the right thing at the right time.

"No, no, I didn't mean it in a bad way. He's . . . healthy looking. That's . . . you know, a good thing, right?" Martin stammers.

The guilt-ridden weekend-father gets defensive.

"This is the first cupcake I've ever given him! I mean, it's the holidays, right? What's the harm?"

"Right, right, of course. Cupcakes are great. They're all the rage lately, right?"

"Do you have kids?" the father challenges Martin.

"No, I don't."

"I thought so. People like you don't understand what it's like."

Oh, great. Now Martin is a *people like you*. Martin doesn't want to be a *people like you*.

"It must be . . . challenging. Parenthood," Martin says, attempting to connect with this man, who probably doesn't see his kid as much as he'd like to. This man who probably thought he'd stay married to whomever it is he married and had this child with. This man who probably thought they'd all spend each and every holiday together by the fire, near the Christmas tree, singing carols and exchanging gifts and making memories. This man who didn't expect to stuff his kid's face with cheap cupcakes in a diner with strangers two days before Christmas. He didn't expect that he would ever have to explain himself to *people like Martin*. Martin is about to reach out his hand to touch this man's shoulder in a gesture that would undoubtedly soothe the moment and bond the two in everlasting friendship.

Except before Martin can reach out to touch him, this man, growing more agitated by the moment, says, "I'll bet you've never experienced a terrible-two tantrum, have you?"

Martin shakes his head. The man sighs heavily and then shakes his finger at Martin challengingly, waving it in Martin's face.

"I get him for three hours tonight. If he wants a cupcake, I'm going to give him a Goddamn cupcake!"

That's when the previously happy, frosting-faced kid bursts out with an ear splitting crying fit. Martin gets up with a "Merry Christmas" and quickly walks away from the friendship that will never be.

He looks around the diner, trying to figure out his next move. He tentatively walks over to a young tattooed couple, who briefly stop making-out to glare at him. The girl has a lizard tat on her forearm. She snarls at Martin. The girl, not the lizard.

Martin turns on his heels and walks to the other side of the diner, where he spots an old-timer enjoying a piece of pumpkin pie. The fact that the old man has pumpkin puree stuck in his mustache doesn't gross Martin out the way it would've in the past. Martin was great at being messy but despised it in others. Now that Martin has cleaned up his act, he's no longer annoyed by the messiness of things. He makes eye contact with the old guy who looks up and smiles. Martin points to his face to let the guy know about the pumpkin in his 'stache. The old guy wipes it away with a napkin and then gives Martin a thumbs-up sign. Martin smiles.

Eve asks Martin if she can get him anything.

"Good pie," says the old man.

"Sounds good," Martin tells Eve.

He sits down at the table next to the old timer. He doesn't want to feel sorry for himself, because it's just so damn cliché to feel like this during the holidays. But as he watches the old man, seemingly happily enjoying his pie, Martin can't help but see himself in this old man. The only thing worse than being middle-aged and alone during the holidays could be being old and alone during the holidays.

Something's got to change.

CHRISTMAS EVE

There's a fantastic black-and-white photo hanging above Elizabeth's fireplace. It's a photo she took of her son, Shane, when he was a baby. He's being nestled in his father's arms in the hammock that hangs from their oak tree in the backyard. Elizabeth was able to capture the strength and beauty of this moment as if it were taken spontaneously, even though she may have set up her subjects just so. She has a gift for sharing stories through her photos, and Martin couldn't be more proud of her. He must remember to have Elizabeth take photos of Rick and Susan's baby girl.

"I still can't get over it. We haven't had a Christmas together in . . . how long has it been, Martin?" Elizabeth asks.

Martin isn't sure how long it's been exactly, but long enough to see that his baby nephew isn't very baby-like anymore. In fact, he talks and walks. Shane must be about eight or so. How could Martin have done this? How could he, by his own choice, have stayed away for so many years? He'd missed birthdays and holidays and being part of the ups and downs of his sister's life. She'd lost their parents, too, and yet she kept . . . living. And what was this great fear of his anyway? Fear of pain? People in pain can eventually move past it, Martin now knows. The sheer, utter lameness of the fact that Martin has been hiding away for so long makes Martin want to shrink away, run, hide again and let Elizabeth have her holiday without him there to muck it up. Except she looks so happy to have him there. He doesn't feel like he's going to muck it up at all. He feels . . . accepted. Loved.

He playfully picks up Shane and throws him over his shoulder.

"Man, you weigh a ton! What are you, all muscle? Are you a body builder or something?" Shane giggles, enjoying this rough-housing with his uncle. Martin's brother-in-law, Thomas, hands Martin a mug of egg-nog.

"So, Martin, Liz told me that you worked on something about quantum physics? I didn't know you were into that sort of thing."

Martin tells them all about the film, the awards and the professor. He thinks about telling them his own, more personal journey with it all, but decides against it. *Baby steps,* he thinks to himself. Professor cuddles up with Martin as Martin explains the multiverse theory.

"Wouldn't that be amazing? If it were possible to actually travel like that?" Elizabeth says.

"Well some people believe that we actually do visit our parallel lives, it's just that we don't remember them," Martin says.

"I wonder what I'm doing in another life," Elizabeth says.

"You're a pilot," Martin blurts out.

"What?"

"I mean . . . didn't you used to say that you wanted to learn how to fly a plane?"

"Oh. Right. I forgot about that."

"How about that, sweetie. You're probably up there flying around this very moment," Thomas jokes.

Shane holds up a wrapped gift from under the tree.

"Can I?" Shane asks.

"Is that the one you want to open tonight?" Elisabeth asks.

"Yeah. It's from Uncle Martin!" Shane says.

"Go for it, kiddo," says Thomas.

Shane tears open the wrapping to discover his gift from Uncle Martin. It's a book. It's *the book*.

"Wow. It's so cool. It looks super old," Shane says.

"What's it about?" asks Elizabeth.

"Possibilities." Martin smiles. The warmth of this moment washes over him and he's certain that his life couldn't possibly get any better than this.

Shane places the book on the coffee table and then gives Martin a big hug. "Thanks, Uncle Martin!"

The book suddenly blows open to page 111. Martin looks around, as if expecting something to happen, but nothing does.

"That's weird. There's no breeze in here," Thomas says.

Shane goes back to the book and studies the pages. He's mesmerized by the drawings.

"Dad. Look how cool."

"Very cool," Thomas agrees as he puts another log on the fire. Elizabeth, smiling ear-to-ear, gives Martin a big hug.

"I'm so glad you're here."

"Me too. Listen, I'm sorry about . . ."

Elizabeth shushes Martin's attempt at an apology with a quick, "More egg-nog?" She grabs his mug and walks off to the kitchen. The doorbell rings. "Are we expecting someone, Thomas?" Elizabeth yells from the kitchen.

"Nope. Not that I know of."

"Maybe it's carolers!" Shane says, jumping up and down in anticipation. "I'll get it!" Shane puts the book back down on the table and rushes to answer the door.

"I'm going to freshen up!" Martin says as he makes his way to the bathroom. As he washes his hands he thinks to himself that he didn't even know carolers still existed. Maybe in small towns, but this isn't so small. He thinks about the Norman Rockwell vibe and thinks that he might like to live in a place that feels like this. A place where a ringing doorbell could mean that instead of someone trying to sell you something, there might be someone wanting to sing you something.

Shane opens the door, where, instead of carolers, stands a beautiful woman, soaked head to toe from the rain. She looks down at Shane and smiles.

"You wouldn't happen to know how to change a tire, would you?"

"I'm too little to change a tire." Shane says.

Elizabeth and Thomas arrive at the door, and the woman explains the situation to them in rapid-fire.

"I'm so sorry to bother you, on Christmas Eve no less, but I was on my way to my parents' house and I was running late, as usual, and my tire blew out. It just went 'POP!' It was so scary, nothing like that has ever happened to me before."

Martin stares into the bathroom mirror. He can't believe his ears. That voice. *No, it can't be.* He splashes cold water on his face. He must be hallucinating. Or maybe, less dramatically, just imagining things. It's Christmas Eve, he's overwhelmed with happy emotions from being reunited with his family. It's natural that his mind would take things further and make him imagine that he's hearing Abby's voice.

Thomas takes the stranger's coat. "I'll be right back with a towel. Come in, come in." Elizabeth leaves for the kitchen. "I'll get you some hot apple cider." The stranger stands there alone with Shane who is now clutching his book to his chest and staring at her.

"I really don't want to be a bother, I'm so . . ." the stranger continues but then stops abruptly when Martin enters the room.

Shane looks at his uncle, who is standing there, frozen, unable to speak.

Shane looks back at the stranger, who is also frozen, unable to speak, staring at his uncle.

Elizabeth comes back with a drink. "Don't be silly. You're not a bother at all."

"It's not your fault about your car. These things happen," adds Thomas, draping a large towel over the stranger.

Elizabeth and Thomas sense the stillness in the room. Confused, Elizabeth asks the stranger, "Is everything okay?" The stranger continues to stare at Martin and Martin continues to stare at the stranger.

Shane breaks the silence. "That's my uncle Martin!"

"Hi, Uncle Martin," the stranger says.

"Hi, Abby," Martin says.

"How did you know her name?" asks Shane.

"Have we met?" Abby says.

Thomas, not sure what the hell is going on, says, "Okay, so let's have a look at that car, shall we?"

"Honey, *Martin* is great with cars. Let him go." Elizabeth winks at her husband to alert him to the fact that there's a spark between her brother and the pretty stranger. Thomas doesn't quite catch his wife's drift.

"Well, honey, I'm pretty handy around automobiles myself. Remember that one time driving back from . . ."

Martin heads straight for the door, grabs an umbrella and asks Abby where her car is.

"This way," Abby quickly says as she heads out the door with Martin right behind her.

Elizabeth turns to her husband. "Seriously? Did you think I had something in my eye just now?" Elizabeth smacks her husband's arm. Shane runs to the window to watch his uncle at work. Elizabeth and Thomas follow him.

"He's going to kiss her!" Shane declares.

"Shane, they just met. Nobody's that smooth," Thomas says.

Martin changes Abby's tire in the pouring rain while she holds the umbrella over him, pointing a flashlight on the tire.

Abby yells over the sound of the rain.

"It's so funny! I wrote a story just like this once! Well, I dreamt it. Then I wrote it. That's how I get most of my ideas!"

"You're a writer?" Martin yells.

"Yes. Sci-Fi comedy romance. It's my hybrid genre!"

Abby, unsure why she feels so familiar with Martin, quizzes him.

"Did you go to Noble High?"

"Nope."

"USC?"

"uh-uh."

"So, you visit your sister around the holidays and I visit my folks every holiday . . . Maybe our paths have crossed around town somehow? Like, at the Walgreens or maybe the movie theatre . . . Do you guys go to the movies on Christmas Day?"

Martin has finished changing the tire. He takes the flashlight from Abby. She now holds the umbrella over the both of them as they stand face to face in the pouring rain.

"God, it's so good to see you again," Martin says.

She feels the connection too, but doesn't understand it.

"*Meet* me, you mean."

Their faces almost touch. They look so deep into each other that Abby feels like she might faint.

154

"I'd really like to see you again," Martin tells her.

"Okay."

"Actually, I'd like to never stop seeing you."

"But, we just met . . . I don't know anything about you."

"You know me better than anyone," Martin tells her as he moves in even closer. Their lips gently touch. Abby is frozen until she lets herself follow her heart, which is screaming at her to just let this happen.

They kiss under the umbrella, and it feels like coming home for them both. Abby doesn't know why, but she doesn't much care about the details at the moment.

"Where have you been?" Abby asks Martin.

"It's a long story."

They continue to kiss under the umbrella, both of them fully aware that there's no other time nor place that they'd rather be than here and now, with each other.

AUTHORS NOTE

The bed and breakfast referred to in this book, *La Tua Casa*, is based on an actual place that I visit each year, *La Ciminiera Country House.*

This gorgeous villa is run by the delightful Giancarlo and Adriana Tomassetti. There's an eco/bio lake, a grotto, a frescoed spa, a fantastic daily breakfast and sunflowers galore.

If you find yourself in Italy, in this, or a parallel life, I highly recommend that you pay them a visit.

Tell them I sent you.

https://www.laciminiera.it/it/country-house.php

On Sale Now!

For more information
visit: www.SpeakingVolumes.us